Critics are saying...

"Wow, sharply written characters, excellent plot, great writing, and more heat than I know what to do with? Sounds like a strong recommend today."
--*Sylvia Storm, E-Read Erotica Reviews*

"I fell in lust, I fell in love. I was turned on. My heart was torn and repaired all within the pages of this marvelous book. ... This was the most beautifully bittersweet story I've ever read. ... Jaret blew me away with her intensely erotic and funny story. ... She's definitely secured a spot on my favorite authors list with Extreme Close-Up. ... I won't be forgetting it anytime soon and I wouldn't want to.
--*Amanda "Hootie" Clark, Globug & Hootie Need a Book blog*

"It was a very satisfying ending. Braden and Lisa's relationship was so, so sexy and wicked, but it was also fulfilling. ... I most definitely recommend Extreme Close-up and also look forward to Lisa's friend Natalie's story, Over-Exposed."
--*Andrea Thompson, The Bookish Babe*

"Extreme Close-Up was one fabulously hot read!"
--*Autumn Davis, Martini Times Romance*

Extreme Close-Up

by
Julie Jaret

He's hot, young... and way off-limits.

<u>Dedications</u>

To my long-suffering and ever-supportive husband: Thanks for always believing in me -- especially when I couldn't believe in myself. You're still a hottie after all these years.

To Jess: You're the best sister in the world and I could never have done it without you. (How was that?)

Chapter One

"TOO DAMN HOT." Lisa Taylor grumbled, stepping away from her camera. If she could have seen the little frown line crinkled above her dark brown eyes, she'd have smoothed it immediately. Not out of vanity, but because that's what women of a certain age have to do. Especially those women whose stubborn last ten pounds of pregnancy weight settled in over the years, so when they look in the mirror they see their mother.

She nudged the box of paperclips a few degrees to the left. Shoving her wavy blonde hair out of the way, she checked the viewfinder again.

"Shit. Could we have *more* glare?" She rubbed her jaw, sore from hours of teeth-clenching.

"Somebody's cheerful today." She heard the clicking of heels on the concrete floor as her best friend, Natalie came around the corner with a greasy bag that smelled delicious.

The studio space Lisa shared in the artsy section of midtown Atlanta may have been an expensive noose around her neck, but the proximity to Nat's law office had its advantages.

"The brainiacs in marketing redesigned all the boxes with a gloss finish that's a bitch to light. They're paperclips. Who gives a rat's ass about the box?"

"Who gives a rat's ass about paperclips?" Natalie unpacked cartons of Chinese take-out and a handful of little sauce packets.

1

"I do. Allegedly." Lisa dug chopsticks into a box of lo mein. "I'm living the dream, taking pictures of thumbtacks and ballpoint pens."

"So maybe it's not always fulfilling. You're still making a living doing what you love. How many people get to do that?" Nat challenged, dumping rice on her plate. "You shoot this crap to pay the bills so you can take the pictures you actually *want* to take."

"Bills," Lisa groaned through a mouthful of noodles. "Don't get me started. They threatened to cut my rates again."

When she had re-entered the job market after her divorce, Lisa was excited to build a career out of her longtime hobby. After a few weeks snapping portraits of screaming brats on Santa's knee, she was even more determined. By the end of a brief stint shooting heavy farm equipment on location, she was desperate. When the big-box office supply chain hired her to shoot their catalogues, she knew she was damn lucky.

Three years later, she still knew she was lucky. And it was still boring as hell. Even worse, she hadn't done any of her own photography in months because, after taking shot after shot of copiers and computers all week, who had the energy to be creative?

Natalie pointed her chopsticks at Lisa, "That reminds me -- my dad and the other partners are looking to get portraits taken for the lobby wall. I recommended you."

"Crusty old lawyers?"

"Granted, they're a little less interesting than the paperclips..."

Lisa crinkled her nose. "I've never shot people, but I guess I could shoot lawyers."

"That's the spirit." Nat raised her egg roll in a toast.

"You don't wanna hear it, so this is me not saying that it's bullshit the 'Wall of Partners' won't include you."

"Thanks. I appreciate your not bringing it up."

"Don't mention it."

After lunch and a soul-cleansing rant, Lisa cracked open her fortune cookie.

IF YOU CAN READ THIS, YOU ARE TOO CLOSE.

Natalie looked over her shoulder. "In bed," she added, opening her own cookie.

"Right. 'Cause reading's one of the two things I ever do in bed these days. What's yours?"

Nat unfurled her own fortune and read, "'Don't forget to play.'"

"In bed," she tacked on.

"With myself, I presume. Unless there's a man in here..." Natalie said, shaking the cookie to no avail. The alarm on her phone bleeped and she shut it off. "Well, that's time." As usual, she had to rush back to work so as not to catch any shit for being gone too long.

As Lisa cleaned up, she admitted to herself that she really was thankful she could make her own hours and, to an extent, do her own thing professionally. The rest of the day, her mood was upbeat. She hardly even grumbled at all while shooting a series of pencil lead refills.

She was surprised when Natalie showed up again the next morning. "Hi, I'm the new intern!"

"Why aren't you at the office? They'll revoke your workaholic's license," she chuckled.

"No worries. I've got nepotism."

Lisa rolled her eyes. "A lot of good that's done you." She snapped one last shot of a tape dispenser and removed it from the light box.

"What do you want next?" Natalie perused the selection. "Ream of paper... two-hole punch... ooh, this is new!" She pushed a handsome, dark-haired man into the light box, which had inexplicably grown and morphed into a white-draped canopy bed. The lighting on the man's chiseled jaw was perfect as he smiled at Lisa and took off his shirt.

"Too hot," she murmured, finding herself beside the hunk on the bed. Then Natalie was gone, the camera was gone, and the god-damned office supplies were gone.

The man's pants were gone, and he was working his way down Lisa's chest, biting the buttons off her shirt as he went. She squirmed and dug her short nails into her palms.

"I don't believe we've met. Do you work with Vance?"

"No. I don't commune with selfish bastards."

Every stitch of Lisa's clothes melted away as the man's mouth made a slow, meandering journey down her belly and beyond. He growled and his breath fanned her most neglected place. As his tongue inched ever closer to contact, his growl grew louder. Unpleasant. Ugly, even.

"Are you shitting me?" Lisa punched her pillow. To someone who'd slept like crap the last few years -- and was just gypped out of an orgasm -- the lawnmower sounded like bottle caps in a blender. "Who the hell is mowing their lawn this early?" Her suburban Dunwoody neighborhood was hardly ever disturbed by lawn mowers on weekday mornings, when practically everyone was at work or yoga.

Hair matted from the restless night, she yanked at the twisted noose of her t-shirt, extricated herself from the snarled bedding and stumbled to the window. Pressing her face to the glass, she scowled out at the world in search of the inconsiderate jackass vying for yard of the month.

As her eyes adjusted to daylight, she caught a glimpse of someone pushing a lawnmower out of view. "What the-- Who the hell's mowing my lawn?"

Cursing the sandman and whoever invented the lawnmower, she pulled on some ratty sweatpants and stomped outside where the fragrance of fresh-cut grass annoyed her even more. She didn't know whose yard the guy was *supposed* to be mowing, but it wasn't her screw-up and she did not have the money to pay some random lawn--

--god.

Lisa stopped dead on the old stone path, perhaps subconsciously remembering it was the "safe zone" back in the days when the kids played tag in her yard. She rubbed her eyes and blinked at the approaching figure whose shirtless, sweat-slicked body made her recent dream man look dumpy. *I really hope I'm awake right now.*

Mirrored sunglasses glinted back at her. The lawn god turned his baseball cap from back to front and shut off the mower.

Lisa braced for confrontation, holding her ground on the overgrown path. The gorgeous young guy bearing down on her was undeterred by the invisible shield of the stones, so she held up a hand to stop him.

"Hey, uh, hate to tell you this, but you're at the wrong house."

"Sorry ma'am. I didn't realize you were home," he mumbled, and tugged off his cap to wipe his brow with a forearm.

She watched a bead of sweat land on his chest, where it slid past a delectably-tight nipple and continued south over the bronze moguls of his belly, disappearing into the waistband of his low-slung cargo shorts...

Jesus, Lisa, stop eye-fucking the kid. She jerked her gaze back to the twin mirrors of his glasses, shielding her eyes as if she had been avoiding the sun's glare just now, not ogling the nether-regions of a boy probably young enough to be her son. *Nice try. Maybe he won't notice the sun is* behind *you.*

"What I'm saying is I didn't hire you. You're mowing the wrong lawn."

"I don't think so. I'll finish up and get out of your way."

"What do you--?" Then it hit her.

Vance.

She could handle a kid who might be annoyed because he mowed the wrong yard and wouldn't get paid, but she was too tired and cranky to deal with her ex-husband's manipulative bullshit. So maybe the adrenaline roaring in her ears masked the sputtering sound of pipes coming to life, or maybe she was so pissed off she just ignored it.

Whatever the reason, she started in on the lawn god with, "Listen, I'm not gonna argue with you," and by the time she demanded to see his work order, she was yelling over the sprinklers as they cycled through, drenching them both.

"I don't actually have a work order, per se."

Lisa couldn't see the eyes behind his water-flecked sunglasses but she felt them, and was uncomfortably reminded that she was braless under the ancient Star Wars t-shirt she'd slept in. She crossed her arms and felt the scrape of chill-tightened nipples on her wrists.

Now waterlogged, the lawn god's low-slung shorts slid lower and she had to force herself not to look directly at his deep V-cut abs, the likes of which she'd only seen on models and movie stars.

Her breathing was ragged. She felt a little lightheaded, and for a second she worried she might faint. Then she realized it was her libido dusting out the cobwebs and lighting up the "open" sign, and decided she would rather pass out. She wasn't any good at this stuff when she was young and skinny, and she sure as hell wasn't even gonna think about it, now.

Those mirrored lenses tilted up again as the spray came back around. "I see you got an irrigation system."

"Nothing gets by you, huh?" Lisa blinked water out of her eyes and caught him stifling a grin. She scowled and trudged back toward the house, "Well I've got an unpleasant phone call to make, since my ex-husband apparently took it upon himself to hire your company."

"No, wait. Ma'am, please."

She plowed on. "So if you insist on mowing the rest of my yard--"

He jogged to catch up with her. "Please stop walking."

"-- you can just tell them to send the bill to that son-of-a-bitch."

"Ah, shit. Mrs. Taylor, wait."

<u>Chapter Two</u>

THE LAWN GOD knew her name.

Lisa froze on the top step as she reached for the door handle. She turned and found herself eye level with his mirrored lenses. Standing this close, she could see burnished gold stubble on his angular jaw. A small, white scar on his chin. Full lips flushed a deep rose topped with a finely-sculpted cupid's bow. Sandy hair overdue for a cut curled from under the faded ball cap. His Adam's apple bobbed, a sign of nerves at odds with the well-muscled hunk of sun-kissed man-boy before her.

She squinted as the sun became too bright for her dilated pupils.

I'm so sex-starved, I could eat this kid alive.

Go for it -- he looks yummy.

Who am I, Mrs. Robinson?

Ignoring her bickering inner voices, she put her hands on her hips. "So, you do have a work order after all."

"Not exactly." His voice was warm and raspy and just as delicious as the rest of him. He reached up to rub his shoulder, bicep flexing across his hard chest. The braided leather around his wrist would've looked like a corny bohemian affectation on anyone else, but Lisa found it sexy as hell.

She caught herself staring. "Uh-huh. You want to tell me how you know my name?" She wracked her brain for any possible way she could have forgotten meeting this person.

"I'm not supposed to. How 'bout I just leave and--"

"How 'bout no?"

He chuckled and ran a hand over his jaw. "Didn't really expect you to go for it." Then he pulled off his glasses.

Those eyes. Like the bottom of the ocean. Dark and deep, not quite green, not quite blue.

"Brady?"

His sheepish smile was familiarly crooked. "Sorry about the cloak and dagger."

Lisa had a hard time reconciling the sexy man on her lawn with Brady Healey, the boy who had spent a good chunk of his childhood drinking iced tea at her kitchen table. He'd been like a big brother to her son, Jake, always there for him and frequently including him in social events, despite their eight-year age difference. When Jake was little, Brady was the only babysitter who could get him to brush his teeth and go to bed on time. Brady taught him how to swing a bat, helped with his math homework, and convinced Jake that eating broccoli wouldn't kill him. Jake was fifteen now, but Lisa knew most of his fondest memories were from the summer vacations the two families would spend together at the old lake house.

But all that was years ago. After Brady got involved with football, he spent less and less time with Jake. Gorgeous and cocky, he had screwed his way through high school on good looks and quarterback cred. In his senior year, he became a local celebrity when ESPN featured him as an all-star college recruit. Lisa remembered how proud Jake was of Brady, even when he was lonely and missing him.

Lisa crossed her arms over her chest. "Does your mother know you're here?" His mother, Elena had been Lisa's best friend, back before shared family vacations became a thing of the dusty past.

"No." He broke eye contact and shook his head, absently rubbing his shoulder again. Lisa remembered hearing he had injured it during a game earlier that year, shortly before he was to graduate from the University of Georgia. The rotator cuff tear was severe enough to end his professional football career before it ever began.

She nodded toward his shoulder. "I was sorry to hear about your injury."

"It happens," he shrugged.

"Yes, but I'm sorry it happened to *you*, Brady."

"Thanks. And it's 'Braden' these days, Mrs. Taylor," he said with a man's grin.

"It's *Ms.* Taylor these days, Braden." Lisa hated how bitter she sounded.

He nodded. "I'm sorry. About... everything."

"It happens," she shrugged with a ghost of a smile.

"Yeah, but it shouldn't have happened to *you*." His eyes went stormy and Lisa had to look away.

As a kid, Brady -- *Braden* -- had had a belligerent streak that came out in defense of those he felt needed protection. Lisa remembered him arguing with his parents when he thought they'd unfairly grounded his older sister, Stephanie. He'd had angry words with Lisa's ex-husband, Vance after hearing him call Jake an idiot for spilling a drink. And he always had zero tolerance for Vance's casual disrespect of Lisa.

Lisa was fresh out of college when she met Vance. He was good-looking and gregarious, always the life of the party. He was only five years older than she, but his personality (and a great economy) had already made him a successful stockbroker. Lisa was proud of him and a few years later, proud of their little family. After earning a photography degree from a school full of art snobs she had learned not to take herself too seriously, so she didn't mind the occasional jokes at her expense. At least, that's what she told herself.

Once, at the lake house when Braden was about sixteen, he overheard Vance tell Lisa to get him a beer. As she walked to the fridge, Braden came in and let the screen door slam behind him.

"Mr. Taylor, I'm sure you didn't mean to set a bad example for Jake and me," Brady said with a muscle ticking in his jaw. *"You meant to say 'get me a beer... what?'"*

"You're right, kid," Vance said, then hollered over his shoulder, *"Get me a beer, bitch!"* Braden's father, Chet, slapped Vance's back and they laughed their asses off. Lisa thought Vance was about to get his teeth knocked in by the overgrown teenager, but Braden left before his temper -- or his dad -- could get the best of him. It embarrassed Lisa to remember how much shit she put up with from

Vance, and how a kid like Brady -- *Braden!* -- saw it long before she did.

Anxious to change the subject, she asked about his plans for summer, and busied herself plucking dead leaves from a blue hydrangea bush.

"I'm tending bar down at Sully's and I might take a couple classes."

"Didn't you just graduate?"

Braden chuckled with uncharacteristic self-deprecation. "Yeah, but what are you gonna do with a bachelor's in biology?" He had a lot to say about why his undergraduate degree was worthless, but Lisa couldn't tell if he was trying to convince her or himself. Either way, he didn't sound like the forward-thinking boy she used to have long talks with on the dock.

It annoyed her that she noticed.

It annoyed her even more to realize it bothered her. She wanted him gone.

"Do you still live on campus?"

"No, I had to move out of the football dorm. I'm crashing at my mom's 'til I find an apartment."

There was an awkward silence as they both pictured Braden living in the house a few streets over with Elena and her new husband, Vance: Lisa's former best friend and her ex-husband.

"So Vance *did* send you to do the lawn. In lieu of rent, knowing him." He started to interject, but Lisa talked over him. "Well, you can tell him I don't need his games or his charity or whatever the hell he's-- Never mind, I'll tell him myself."

"Hang on," Braden grabbed her wrist. "It wasn't Vance. Just let me finish and we'll forget it, okay?"

"No. Not okay." She tried to tug her arm free, but his grip was like iron. "I realize I'm kinda hyper-focusing on the lawn-mowing, but he's pulled this crap before, plus, I stayed home to take a mental health day which I *really* needed, and so far it's having the total opposite effect!"

He let her arm drop. "It was Jake. Don't tell him I told you. Please."

"Jake? My son, Jake?"

"Yeah."

"He's away at baseball camp."

"I know. He's worried about you, but he'd be pissed if he knew I told you that. He asked me to sneak in while you're at work and take care of your yard and stuff while he's away."

Lisa was stunned. "I didn't know you guys were in touch."

"We weren't. It was a surprise when he called. A good surprise. I missed him."

"He missed you, too." Lisa's eyes welled up and she couldn't hold back a watery smile. "God, I love that little shit. I can't believe he did that."

"He's a good kid. Best little brother a guy could ask for." His smile fell. "You're not gonna tell him about this conversation, are you?"

"No. I promise," she said shaking her head. "And since we've established that Vance had nothing to do with it, I'm going to pay you for your work."

He flashed a devastating grin. "No ma'am, you're not."

She tried to argue, but all he would accept from her was a glass of iced tea.

Back inside, Lisa went straight to the bathroom to peel off her wet clothes. She climbed into a steamy shower with a riot of thoughts.

Jake... such a sweetheart...

Acting like a high school girl, drooling over Brady Healey.

It's Braden these days.

That body... good god.

She chuckled when she realized her bath puff had been working between her legs for quite a while.

Well, look who's awake.

So this is "horny." Yeah. I remember this.

I really need to get laid.

What if I'd hit on him before I knew who he was? Christ, Vance would've had a field day with that.

What if I'd hit on him and he took me up on it? Young guys like him are always horny...

Lisa wiped the fog from the glass shower door and frowned at her reflection in the mirror across the room. *I'd have died of embarrassment.* At forty-one years old, her no-longer-twenty-five-year-old body was still an unpleasant shock whenever she had the unfortunate occasion to get a glimpse of it. *Fuck.*

Naturally blonde and petite, vanity had been a non-issue for most of her life -- a genetic luxury she appreciated more in retrospect. She still had gorgeous skin and wavy, shoulder-length hair of a hundred shades of blond. Even with the weight she'd put on since college, people always assumed she was five or ten years younger than she was.

Regardless, she avoided the mirror and would continue to do so. She wasn't ready to look good for her age.

Chapter Three

"*CHUBBY*?'" NATALIE GROWLED. "You did not just say that."

They were in Lisa's cozy home office. She shrugged without looking up from her computer, where she was color correcting a photograph of manila folders. "I calls 'em as I sees 'em."

"Then you have funhouse mirrors in your bathroom."

"Now, that would be cool."

But Natalie wasn't finished. "Nobody with two eyes and a functional brain would look at *you*--" she made the universal hand gesture for an hourglass figure, "--and think of Jenny-freaking-Craig."

Lisa laughed. She appreciated that Natalie wanted her to feel better about herself, but her willowy friend didn't have post-childbirth hips or boobs that waxed and waned with the moon. She saved the edited photo of manila folders and opened the next: yellow legal pads.

Natalie fell quiet, looking through Lisa's portfolio. The photos included anything and everything -- plants, railings, storefronts, fire hydrants. With colors popping, most were taken very close-up to accentuate texture and depth. Some were shot so tight, it was nearly impossible to identify the subject of the picture. She stopped to study a photo of something pale, smooth and curvy.

"Should I be concerned that this one's kinda turning me on?"

"Only if you have an aversion to butternut squash," Lisa grinned, "but still, you should probably get out more."

Natalie snorted. "Hello, I'm Kettle. Have we met?"

"Yeah, yeah. Point taken."

"My dad needs to see these. Can I borrow this?" Natalie patted the photo book.

"Go ahead. So, they haven't hired anyone to do the portraits?" Lisa tried to hide her relief. Her bank account had dropped below the "art vs. commerce" threshold, and she was considering offers from lenders who wanted her soul.

"Not yet, but I think this will help them decide," Natalie closed the book. "If you can make vegetables look human, imagine what you could do for attorneys."

Lisa laughed.

Natalie didn't. "I wasn't joking."

Lisa felt a little better about her chances for survival as she walked Natalie to the door. At least she did, until Natalie stepped outside and gasped.

"Oh my. You hired a gardener?" They stared across the yard to where Braden was clipping a hedge, mouthwatering even at a distance. "Suddenly the view from my high-rise condo holds much less appeal."

They watched him stretch to cut a long branch overhead. His broad, sweat-glistened back tapered to a narrow waist, then flared to a hint of rounded ass where his shorts hung low. Lisa had the unwelcome thought that his shorts were probably not the only thing that hung low on him.

"That's Elena's son, Braden."

"No shit?"

"Yeah. He's all grown up, now."

"I noticed."

Braden must've felt their eyes on him. He froze a moment then looked over and smiled, raising the clippers in greeting. Lisa waved back.

"As your lawyer and best friend, it's my expert opinion that you should totally hit that."

She looked at her friend and snorted, "Right. You're insane."

"Eye for an eye," Natalie shrugged as they turned down the stone path toward the driveway.

"He's twenty-three. I've got clothes older than that," Lisa argued. "Nothing that fits, but still."

As soon as Natalie's car disappeared from view, Lisa went back inside and poured a tall glass of iced tea for Braden. When she brought it out to him, he stopped bagging cuttings and took off his sunglasses. She was dressed in old cut-offs and a t-shirt since she was working from home today, and in the heartbeat before his eyes met hers, she could've sworn his warm gaze flickered over the rest of her.

"Is that for me?" His smile made Lisa's mouth go dry.

"Yes, and you're doing too much," she said, handing him the glass. With the condensation left on her hand, she patted her face and neck in a futile effort to cool down.

"I disagree. Respectfully," he said, accepting the tea and holding it up in a toast to her. He drank deeply, downing half the glass in one draw. "Thanks, Ms. Taylor. You know I've always loved your iced tea." He licked his lips.

"I remember, but I wish you'd let me pay you in something other than tea."

Braden's pupils dilated like he was locked onto prey, and Lisa immediately realized how bad that sounded. Well, it sounded pretty *good*, but it wasn't something she would ever intentionally say. Especially not to him.

"Shit. That came out wrong," she said with an embarrassed laugh.

Braden melted her with a grin and handed her the empty glass. "Thanks again for the tea." His eyes were still dark as they disappeared behind his sunglasses.

When Lisa brought the glass inside, she opted to hand-wash it instead of putting it in the dishwasher. Because saving water and energy was good for the planet. She couldn't help that the kitchen window looked out over the yard.

That evening after dinner, she was trying and failing to keep her mind on her work (color correcting photos of mechanical pencils) when the doorbell rang. En route to answer it, she caught a glimpse of a broad shoulder and muscled arm through the sidelight window sheer. She'd been resolute in her determination not to trot back outside with more tea that afternoon, and now she scolded herself for wishing she had time to change out of the cut-offs and tee she'd had on all day.

Why the palpitations?   It's just Brady Healey, Elena and Chet's son.

Jake's babysitter.

Vance's step-son.

She was able to get her breathing under control in time to open the door.

"Hi," she smiled. "It's only been like five hours. Nothing grows that fast, not even my weed farm back there." She leaned a hip against the doorjamb and tried to look relaxed, like any other mom chatting with an old friend of her son. She hoped he hadn't been reading her mind all afternoon.

Braden grinned, those gorgeous eyes twinkling at her. "I wouldn't be so sure, but that's not why I'm here."

"No?" Lisa noticed he ends of his hair were wet and he smelled of woodsy soap. Something long-dormant stirred awake in her core.

"Do you know when you last changed your air filter?"

She blinked. "Oh. They probably did it when I had my oil changed, why?"

"I mean the one in your house."

"There's one in my house?"

He chuckled. "Yeah."

Lisa let him in and followed him down the hall to an air vent thingie she had passed a million times and never really noticed. She was mortified when he removed the cover and pulled out a big flat square of filth.

"Oh my god! How did you know?"

"Lucky guess." Braden put the filter back and promised to pick up a replacement the next day. Once again he refused to accept Lisa's money, but as he tightened the screws on the vent she slid her last $20 into his back pocket.

"That was disgusting. Guess it's one of the things Vance used to take care of." She saw Braden's mouth tighten at the mention of her ex-husband's name.

"If you ask me, Vance didn't take care of the right things." He stood, brushing off his hands. "Not that you asked me."

Even back when he was just a beautiful boy, Lisa felt something in Braden's eyes was disconcertingly *knowing*. He locked them on her now, and she remembered why she often avoided eye contact with him when he was a kid. Because he made her never want to look away.

She faked a chuckle and turned down the hall. "It's okay. I'm not exactly president of his fan club, either." That was the understatement of the decade, but she had wasted enough hours bitching about Vance to Natalie and anyone else who would listen. She didn't need to unload it all again on his stepson.

Braden followed her to the door. "It'll be good to have a break from him for a few weeks."

"Oh, he's back in the New York office?" During her marriage, Lisa and Jake had had the house to themselves for weeks at a time when Vance traveled for work. In the beginning, she even missed him. Now she wondered if he had actually left town at all.

"No, vacation. They're going to Europe."

Lisa gave a harsh laugh. "For three weeks? You're kidding." For the better part of their marriage, she'd tried to persuade Vance to go to Europe, but he insisted he had no interest in traveling outside the U.S. Not to mention, "He said his last child support payment was late because they had to get some work done on the house."

Braden scowled, "Well yeah, if by 'having to get some work done' he meant gutting and remodeling the kitchen with the SubZero my mom had to have." He was clearly angry at Vance and Elena on Lisa's behalf and it made her want to hug him.

She backed a step away. "Ah, Elena..." she smiled ruefully.

"You must hate her." He was watching closely for a reaction, so Lisa simply shrugged.

"I thought I did, but really I just hated the situation. She is who she is."

"She's a spoiled brat."

"She's your mom," Lisa said firmly, because she thought she should.

"You're not disagreeing."

"No, I'm not. She's a brat."

His answering grin was way too sexy for Lisa's own good. She knew he would be repulsed if he had any idea how her body was responding to him, how very *aware* of him she was.

She thought back to the boy he was and remembered, "You were a pretty big brat, too, as I recall."

He laughed, nodding. "Yeah, I can see why you'd think so. I had my reasons."

Lisa imagined those reasons had something to do with football and/or the legions of girls who had followed him around as long as she'd known him. She was going to say as much, but he'd gone quiet. *He probably wants to get the hell out of the depressing old lady's house.*

She opened the door, schooling her face as she smiled up at him, "Braden, thanks for all your--"

"Did you ever fuck my dad?"

The blurted question came out like it had simmered on the stove too long and suddenly boiled over. In the deafening silence that followed, Lisa got the impression he hadn't intended to speak the words aloud. Frozen with her hand on the doorknob, she had about a million follow-up questions, but bit them all back.

"No." With relief, she dropped the facade of polite distance and relaxed. "You want some tea?"

"I'd take a beer," he grinned. A *man's* grin.

She considered a moment, then closed the door and led him to the kitchen.

Chapter Four

LISA HANDED BRADEN an icy bottle and opened another for herself.

"Hope Blue Moon is okay."

"It's great, thanks."

Lisa braced herself for eye contact -- or what she now thought of as "the eye thing." She didn't fool herself that she was anything special, but when he looked at her it felt like she was the only other person on the planet, and like some part of him entered through her eyes, swirled down deep in her body, and licked her clit from inside. And if she were to be totally honest (which she wasn't ready to do just yet), the boy he'd been did the eye thing to her, too.

So she was disappointed -- er, *relieved* -- when instead, he crossed the kitchen for a closer look at a framed photograph on the wall. She took a swallow of the cold beer and closed her eyes in a moment of bliss. This six-pack had probably been in her fridge the better part of a year, since drinking alone was stigmatic and depressing. Opening her eyes, she found him still studying the photo.

"It's a park bench."

"How can you tell?" He cocked his head at the colorful lines and twisted shadows.

"I took it when I visited a friend in Austin a while ago."

"You took this?" Braden glanced at the scribbled signature in the bottom corner, then turned those inquisitive eyes on her. "I love it. It looks like something that should be hanging in a gallery."

"Thanks," Lisa beamed and tried not to squirm. He had zapped both her clit and her ego in one shot that time.

"Do you have any more?"

"Beer?"

"No, more pictures like this."

Before she knew it, they were in up in her office. She leaned against her desk and toyed with the wet label on her beer, watching him make his way around the room from one framed photo to the next. The portfolio Natalie borrowed included all of these and a lot more, and for a moment she regretted lending it out.

Braden stopped to study the voluptuous squash that had turned Natalie on earlier. He turned a sly look at Lisa and grinned, "Wish I was there when you took this one, Ms. Taylor."

She held a straight face. "Oh? So you're a big fan of squash, then?"

"*Squash?*" He laughed, cocking his head for a different perspective. "That's awesome. Guess I'm a big fan of *this* squash, anyway."

"I'd introduce you, but she's long gone. Sucks, 'cause you guys could've been really good together."

Braden grinned and dropped onto her old red velour sofa. She had bought it for her first apartment, long before she met Vance. It was outdated enough to be called "retro" and was really too big for her office, but the more Vance pushed her to get rid of it, the more tightly she'd hung on.

"I love the way you see things," he said, unknowingly doing the eye thing as he tipped back his beer.

Lisa was getting used to breathing normally, despite the throb he caused between her legs. Good thing, too, because the only thing more embarrassing than a middle-aged woman hot for a guy half her age would be the horrified look on his face if he knew.

He gestured with his bottle, "So this is what you do? You take these great pictures and... what? How does it work? I bet you sell a ton of them." His free hand absently petted the soft velour on the sofa arm, and Lisa found herself jealous of a piece of fucking furniture.

"I wish. They're up on a few stock photo websites, but sales are weak. I photograph office equipment and supplies for catalogues. That's my real job." Her attempt to inject some enthusiasm into the words failed miserably.

"Sounds like you meant to say your 'real *boring* job.'"

"Maybe so," Lisa laughed, "but I can take the most gorgeous picture of pencil erasers you'll ever see. How 'bout you?"

He grinned. "Selfies on my phone, that's about it for me."

She sat at the other end of the sofa. "You know what I mean. What's next for you?"

"Hell if I know," he sighed. He had been nursing his beer, but downed half of it now. "I wanted to go into sports medicine, but I was probably concussed when I thought of it."

"Don't bullshit me, Brady. *Braden*. You didn't major in biology by accident."

He wiped a sheepish grin off his face with a big hand. "Damn, I missed you, Ms. Taylor. You're still the only one who never bought the act."

She raised her eyebrows and waited for him to continue.

He stared at the beer dangling from his fingers and took a deep breath. "I've always loved the game of football, ever since I started playing Pop Warner when I was five. I broke my arm for the first time when I was seven -- landed on it in the end zone and the ball rolled away from me. The clock ran out and we lost and I never heard the end of it." A muscle ticked in his jaw before he polished off the beer. "In middle school, I could look at an x-ray of my shoulder and tell you which tendon was strained or torn. By high school, I'd sprained or broken most of my fingers, broken the other arm, strained my Achilles and had shoulder tendonitis."

Jake had dragged Lisa to some of Braden's high school games and she recalled the intensity with which he played. She'd felt it all the way up in the stands. "I remember the arm," she nodded. "Jake was so excited you let him be the first to sign your cast."

"Of course I did," he smiled with a matter-of-fact shrug, like there was never any question. "High school was crazy. I came in as backup quarterback for varsity, but then the seniors got busted at that party and coach bumped me to starter..." His smile faded. "I'd never seen my dad so happy. Not even at Steph's wedding."

Lisa had attended Braden's sister's wedding. In fact, she and Vance had been seated at Elena and Chet's table along with Stephanie's new in-laws. Stephanie was a pretty girl and a beautiful bride who took after her mother in both looks and demeanor. Lisa didn't know her well, as she was five years older than Braden and had her own social life by the time the families became friends.

And it was only a couple months after Stephanie's wedding when Vance and Elena broke up their respective families and came out with their affair. *Good times...*

Lisa's jaw hurt and she realized she was clenching.

Braden continued, "So of course, I kept working and training, and when I got to UGA they started me at quarterback after two games." He shook his head at the memories. "For a while, I thought I'd won and lost everything on that field."

"Not anymore?"

"No. I still love the game of football, but the *job* of football sucks. I hated it. That last tackle did me a favor."

Lisa was enjoying the conversation, and the twelve ounces of beer in her system felt pretty good. She took his empty bottle and asked, "Want another?"

He rocked her with a half-smile. "Sure, if you're not sick of me yet."

"Not yet," she shrugged.

They took their fresh beers to the family room and sat on adjacent sides of the sectional. Lisa picked up the conversation thread. "Okay, so have you applied to med school or what?"

"Med school?" Braden's laugh sounded forced. "I was thinking of physical therapy, not med school."

"And I was thinking you were done trying to bullshit me."

He winced. "Habit. Sorry." He slid off the couch to sit against it on the plush area rug. "Yes, I'd love to go to med school, and no, I haven't applied. My grades in core classes were good enough, but I bombed the MCAT -- you know, the admission exam."

"Huh," she lowered herself to the floor and pulled down a cushion to lean on. "That's the first thing you've said that surprised me."

"That's what happens when you don't study."

"So take it again."

"I was gonna..." He broke eye contact and studied his beer. "But c'mon. I'm smart for a jock, but I'm no med student."

"Never thought I'd hear Chet's voice come out of your mouth."

Braden chuckled. "My dad did say it first, yeah."

"God, he's an asshole." Almost two beers down, the words were out before it occurred to Lisa not to say them. "Oops. Sorry." She felt a little bad about it. Well, not really.

"No, you're right. He is."

"Can't believe you thought I slept with him."

"More like I wanted to be sure you didn't."

"He's just such a..."

Braden laughed. "An asshole, yeah. But that doesn't mean he's wrong."

"Okay maybe it doesn't exactly follow logically, like 'Chet's an asshole, *ergo*, he's wrong about whether you're med school material.' But he still is."

He stared at her face, considering her over the bottle as he took a long swallow.

Lisa felt the throbbing down below and pressed her thighs together. For once, she was thankful for her dark brown eyes, knowing they helped camouflage the lust that dilated her pupils.

He lowered his bottle. "I remember those conversations we used to have. Kinda like this. You were always the one person who'd talk to me... listen to me. Everyone else only cared about the quarterback."

"I saw that."

"We had some marathons, huh? Up at the lake?"

Lisa remembered all too well. "Vance picked a fight with me after one of those marathon talks." She caught herself clenching her jaw again. "He accused me of flirting with our best friends' kid."

His eyebrows shot up. "With me? You did not," he scowled. "Vance is an asshole, too. For many reasons."

"That he is," Lisa grinned and rubbed her jaw.

Braden frowned. "What's that about? Do you have TMJ?"

"No," she shrugged. "I just clench my teeth a lot when I'm stressed."

He nodded. "Right. That's TMJ." He moved closer, but stopped with his fingers mere inches from her face. "Do you mind?"

She shook her head because she didn't trust her voice with him kneeling this close and smelling this good.

He expertly walked his fingers along the edges of her jaw and up almost to her cheekbones then pressed lightly with his thumbs. "Is this where it hurts?"

"Yes."

He massaged small circles with his thumbs, cradling her head in his hands. "These are your masseter muscles and they run from here--" He placed his thumbs above her cheekbones and smoothed them down to the bottom edges of her jaw, "--down to here."

Lisa was dimly aware of him explaining bone structure, and where and how to massage to relieve the ache in her jaw. She was even aware enough to be impressed with his knowledge and manner. Mostly, she was aware of the way his Cupid's bow dimpled his top lip and how it moved as he spoke. And she noticed that the pulse in her clit was like a heartbeat and she briefly wondered if it was somehow *his* heartbeat traveling from his thumbs, through her face and down into the wet crotch of her panties. And she also realized she was breathing very deeply, because when she did she could smell the spice of his skin behind that woodsy soap.

And then he brushed a thumb across her lips and she stopped breathing altogether.

Chapter Five

LISA PULLED AWAY, overriding every desire and instinct to eat him alive, starting with that reckless thumb. She knew Braden had a reputation as a flirt and a tease, but she had always assumed he kept it to age-appropriate girls. No doubt he would be a lot more careful around middle-aged ladies in the future if he knew how close he'd just come to being mauled. She shoved a blonde curl behind her ear and coughed a laugh.

"What do you think you're doing?"

Braden's smile was mischievous. "I'm not a kid anymore, Ms. Taylor."

He sounded half serious, and Lisa silently berated her body for its immediate damp response.

"Right. From what I've heard of your exploits in high school and college, you've got no reason to flirt with the likes of me." She took their empty bottles and stood, hoping he would get the hint and leave before it became obvious what he was doing to her.

He followed her into the kitchen. "Don't believe what people say. I didn't hook up with every girl in school."

Lisa eyed him skeptically.

"Only the blondes with big brown eyes," he winked.

She dropped the bottles in a recycle bin under the sink. Luckily, she was already next to the bin, because she would have dropped the bottles, regardless. "Not that it matters what I think, but was that supposed to convince me you're not a player?" He was so damned sexy and adorable, the only thing she was convinced of was that he had probably nailed every girl in school and some of the teachers, too.

He actually looked embarrassed. "All right, I was kind of a player. *Was*. But I did skew heavily toward brown-eyed blondes."

"That must've been limiting. We're sort of a rare breed."

"Yeah, well... I've always had a thing for your breed." He leaned against the counter and flicked his eyes to meet hers. "For you, specifically."

Lisa blinked, "Uh, what?"

He chuckled. "You must've known I had a crush on you. I was so obvious."

"Nope. I had no clue." She shuddered to imagine how horribly she'd have fucked up his idyllic memories of that innocent crush if she had acted on her impulses earlier.

"Why'd you think I hung out with Jake so much when I was twelve and he was only like, four? I love the guy, but back then he was just an excuse to spend time here."

She leaned a hip against the counter by the sink. "It never crossed my mind. Guess you weren't as transparent as you think." Most likely, she had been so happy for some time to herself, she never stopped to wonder why the older boy enjoyed Jake's company so much.

"I always imagined coming by one day, and sweeping you off your feet."

She smiled. "Aw... that's cute. Where was Vance in this scenario?"

"He got hit by a bus." They laughed and he continued, "So, naturally I stopped by to pay my respects."

"Naturally."

"Then everyone else left and I stayed to help you put all the casseroles in the fridge."

"That was very thoughtful of you." She started to chuckle, but instead almost swallowed her tongue when he closed the distance between them, effectively trapping her against the counter.

"And then I hugged you, like this..." Those well-muscled arms she had privately drooled over skimmed her ribcage and wrapped around her back, pulling her just close enough that her breasts brushed his hard chest. "And kissed your cheek, like this..."

Lisa tightened her hands into fists at her sides, digging her nails into her palms as he pressed soft, warm lips to her cheek... then her jaw... then the sensitive skin behind her ear.

"And I promised to make you forget about that asshole. And you said, 'I already have.'" His lips brushed her ear, making her shiver. She put her hands against his chest and gently pushed him away.

"That's how you envisioned sweeping me off my feet when you were *twelve*?"

He flashed a deep-dimpled grin, though his eyes remained dark and predatory. "The fantasy evolved over time. That might've been more what I had in mind when I was eighteen."

She wondered if it was possible to die from "the eye thing," and she held her breath as his appreciative gaze raked her from head to toe and back again. Somewhere in the back of her mind, she applauded herself for shaving her legs this morning. Unfortunately, as beautiful as he was, and as much as she was dying to enjoy him in ways that were downright illegal in most southern states, there were too many better reasons for that not to happen.

Before she could put the words together to say as much, he slid a big hand behind her neck, licked his lips and pulled her close. "Let me show you what I have in mind at twenty-three."

Lisa backed off, making sure to get more than an arm's length from him. "Braden, I'm sorry, but I'm not interested in you that way."

He relaxed against the counter, crossed his arms and gave her a pointed look. "I thought we didn't bullshit each other." A small smile softened the words. "I'm not ashamed to admit I want you. Why pretend you don't feel the same?"

Ignoring the rush of wet lust in her panties, she insisted, "I'll admit you're very attractive, but that doesn't mean I want you like that."

"With all due respect, Ms. Taylor, your eyes and your body say you do."

"Pardon me?" She wouldn't have responded had she not been so totally caught off-guard by his comment.

"Your pupils are dilated; you're breathing like you just ran up the stairs; your cheeks are flushed; and..." His own darkened eyes dipped down to her breasts.

She didn't have to look to know her nipples were hard. And now they tightened even more for him, the traitors. Humiliated, she crossed her arms over her chest. "I'm not having this conversation."

"There's nothing to be embarrassed about, it's just your body's involuntary response to certain stimuli. It's physiology. Happens to everyone." Before she could interrupt, he asked, "Do you remember at the lake house once, about ten years ago, I pitched a fit and ruined the whole day?"

"'*Once?*'"

He chuckled. "Yeah, I know. I was a brat."

"And what's that got to do with my wanting to crawl under a rock and die right now?"

"I'm thinking of one tantrum in particular. My dad was giving me shit because I had a hard-on, which, of course was my body's involuntary response to certain stimuli. It happened a lot back then, and dad never missed an opportunity to call me out on it."

"Asshole," she muttered.

"That day, the stimulus occurred when Jake was grabbing at you, trying to get you to pick him up. Your bikini top slipped for a second, and I got my first glimpse of a nipple."

"Oh god," She gasped from a mixture of embarrassment and something else.

"Five minutes later, dad caught me starching a sock and decided to be a complete dick about it."

"I'm sorry," she winced. "For what it's worth, though, I appreciate your telling me. Nobody's ever starched a sock in my honor before."

He laughed at her. "Yeah they have, trust me."

Lisa felt her face flush. "Oh. Well, no one else ever told me about it."

"Maybe no one else has been out of his skull in lust with you for half his life." He took a deep breath at the same moment Lisa lost all ability to breathe.

"Braden, I'm beyond flattered, but there's Jake... and everything else. You know this can't happen."

His eyes and voice were dark as sin as he inched closer, "I know we're both adults, both single. I know I'm dying to touch you. I know I can make you feel good."

"Are you trying to kill me?" she whispered.

"I know I have to see that nipple again, because every one I've seen since has paled in comparison."

That brought Lisa back to Earth -- she could only imagine how many sets of boobs he'd seen since then! She rolled her eyes. "That's a joke, right?"

"Nope." He shook his head and pointed at the hardened peak of her left breast. "That, right there, is the nipple that launched a thousand starched socks." He reached for her hand and she jumped away, ass smacking into the cabinet door. With a wry grin, he added, "And now, I'm gonna go home and starch one more."

He placed a chaste kiss on her palm and folded her fingers over it. Then he took the knuckle of her thumb into his hot mouth and released it after a brief but glorious assault by his teeth and tongue. "Make that two more" he rasped.

Lisa sagged against the counter. "You are. You're trying to kill me."

Braden adjusted himself. "The feeling's mutual, Ms. Taylor," he said with a tight smile.

Chapter Six

TWENTY MINUTES AFTER Braden left, Lisa was still sitting with her back against the front door. Her dazed brain struggled to process the night's revelations. Every word, look and touch from him made her feel both beautiful and hideous, simultaneously. *How was that possible?*

Even if she were tempted -- which she wasn't! -- she could never go through with it. It would be impossible enough to measure up to girls his age, let alone his blown-out-of-proportion memory of her younger (thinner, firmer) self. Horny as she was, she was definitely not a masochist. Her knees cracked when she finally stood up and returned to the living room.

She couldn't stop thinking about "the slip." It may have been a decade ago, but the embarrassment was as fresh as if it had happened the moment he told her. She had never been the type to flash for Mardi Gras beads or enter a wet t-shirt contest, so the only men who had ever seen her breasts outside an exam room were Vance and a few previous boyfriends.

As she replaced couch cushions and turned out the lights, the mental movie created when Braden described that long-ago day played over and over in her mind. Her embarrassment ratcheted higher with each loop, causing a strange fight-or-flight type of response: her heart raced, she was short of breath, and there was a throbbing pulse in her clit.

Turning out the lights en route to her bedroom, she was surprised to realize, *you're turned-on, you sick bitch.* She undressed for bed, knowing she would think of Braden every time she wore those cut-offs in the future. And for a change, she felt not just horny, but *sexy*.

Then she made the unfortunate mistake of glancing in the mirror.

And as with any other train wreck, she couldn't look away. Her ample breasts (courtesy of her paternal grandmother's side of the family, despite neighborhood gossip) were succumbing to gravity. Her formerly small waist was now average, at best. And with her rounded ass and hips, she was nothing but a Rubenesque divorcee in a Yoga-butt world. She yanked a huge t-shirt over her head and covered the offensive curves with relief.

It was after eleven, so she climbed into bed and tried to sleep, but it soon became clear it was not gonna happen. Visions of Braden -- both young and less-young -- were doing "the eye thing" in her head. *Fuck it.* She sat up and reached for her laptop.

An hour later, after responding to Jake's email from baseball camp (he hadn't mentioned Braden, so neither did she), taking care of the few bills she could afford to pay, and reading two chapters of a novel without retaining a word, she killed the light and hoped she was tired enough to tune out the words and pictures in her head. But of course, she wasn't. The hottest man she'd ever seen could very well *right now* have his cock in his fist and be thinking sexy things about her.

When had she ever been that tired?

Nobody's ever been that tired.

She got comfortable and in the spirit of "if you can't beat 'em, join 'em," allowed the images in. Maybe she couldn't have him in real life, but here in the dark of her own mind she could be what he thought she was. What she wished she were.

Her fingertips became his eyes as they skimmed across her breasts and teased her tight left nipple. *The one he saw.* Her body responded to her conjured version of him with the same damp heat and soul-deep ache she felt when he was there. For the first time since college, she brought herself to orgasm with only her hands and her mind.

* * *

The next day, Natalie asked Lisa to meet her for happy hour at the pub near the law office. Lisa found her at their favorite table in the back corner.

"Hey girlie," Natalie gave her a quick hug.

"Hey yourself. What's up?"

Natalie smiled as a cute young waitress with a nose ring and a sleeve of colorful tattoos set down a pitcher of beer and filled two icy mugs.

"Enjoy, ladies. Holler if you need anything else." They thanked her as she rushed off.

Natalie grinned at Lisa and lifted her mug. "To you."

She tapped her beer to Natalie's. "For what?"

Natalie slid a check across the table. "For this. Guess what, you're hired. My dad's assistant will call you to set it up."

It wasn't a life-altering check, but it would certainly chip away at some debt. "I'll drink to that," she grinned. "Thanks, Nat. No wonder you're a lawyer; you're pretty damned persuasive."

"Wasn't me. They loved your work. Actually, if I can hang onto the portfolio a little longer, I think you might sell a few prints."

Lisa nodded. "Yeah, sure. That's fine." She didn't need the portfolio back right away. Maybe she'd wished she had it last night when Braden was admiring her work, but she wasn't going to invite him in again.

They drank in thoughtful silence, something Lisa would've found unusual if she weren't the cause of it. She blinked when she realized she had finished her beer.

"Look who's back." Nat fixed her eagle eye on Lisa. "Something you want to tell me?"

"Jesus, no."

"Something I'd *want* you to tell me?"

She grimaced. "Totally."

"Let's have it." Natalie refilled both beers.

Lisa took a deep breath. "Braden came by last night."

"You boinked him!"

"No, but he wanted to."

"Yes!"

"No! It's just-- no. There's Jake and Vance and Elena... it's too complicated."

"Then don't invite Jake and Vance and Elena."

Lisa glared at her over her mug. "I'm serious."

"So am I," Nat said urgently. "If they're in your head, they're in your bed." Then she snorted, adding, "That wasn't supposed to rhyme."

"It's catchy," she smiled. "But there's more to it than that." Last night, she had masturbated with both present-day Braden and young Brady in mind. *Who would do that?* Something was very wrong with her.

Natalie put her persuasive lawyering skills to work. "For fuck's sake, just tell me what happened."

Lisa told her about Braden's visit and what he said, and Natalie listened quietly until she was done, except for one brief interjection ("Wait. You were blessed with tits like those and you've never flashed them? Sorry. Ignore me. Go on.").

She finally finished talking and signaled the waitress for another round.

Natalie fanned herself. "I understand why you're conflicted, but it's not like your families will all be sharing a lake house again anytime soon. You're single adults who are attracted to each other. Why not enjoy that?"

"Because I *can't* enjoy it."

"I saw the guy, Lise," Natalie smirked. "I don't think you'd have a choice."

Lisa shrugged. "Wanna go bowling this weekend?"

"What? You know I hate bowling."

"Why?"

"'Cause I suck at it."

"But there's this new state-of-the-art bowling alley with a bar and light show."

"I'm not gonna bowl any better on a nicer lane. And why'd you jump off topic?"

"I didn't," Lisa said firmly.

She let Natalie stare her down, while the waitress swapped their empties for a new pitcher and filled two new icy mugs.

As soon as they were alone again, Natalie pounced, "So, what am I to glean from your cryptic bowling analogy? That you think you're bad at sex?"

Lisa cringed and looked around to be sure no one heard that, although the pub was so loud, she could hardly hear Natalie, herself. "I know I am, yeah."

"Wild shot in the dark, here... was Vance the kind soul who clued you in on the state of things?"

"He mentioned it, but he wasn't the only one. Even with previous boyfriends, I've never been able to loosen up enough."

"How so? Are you uncomfortable vocalizing? 'Cause you know real people don't usually scream and moan like porn stars."

There was no getting out of this conversation, Lisa realized with a sigh. She drained her mug and stifled a burp as Nat refilled it. "It's more the talk happening inside my head that's the problem."

This was not a subject Lisa was used to discussing, but she tried to explain. Ever since the first boyfriend who got her shirt off and finagled a hand down her pants, she had always worried about how she looked, smelled, tasted. Every sexual experience was couched in embarrassment for her, so she couldn't relax. She had no real reason to worry; body odor was never an issue for her, and when she was young her skin was firm over those excessive curves. Through the years her reasons for worrying changed with her body, but the overall effect stayed the same.

"I'm so hyperaware of myself, I can't be spontaneous. I can't let go."

Natalie's brow wrinkled. "Is that strictly with company? Or alone, too?"

Lisa felt her face redden, and she tried to stifle a grin. "Strictly with company."

"Ah. You had a go after he left." She tipped her mug to Lisa and took a swig. "This isn't my area of expertise, but whatever gets you there when you're alone, I bet it'd work when you've got company, too."

<u>Chapter Seven</u>

WHAT GETS HER there when she's alone?

That seemed like something she should know.

As she photographed items for the back-to-school circular, Lisa thought back on last night's conversation and had to concede Nat had a point. While she never intended to act on her craving for Braden, she did hope to have sex again one day. It was time to look closely at what lit her up.

She snapped a few test shots and checked the results. "Definitely not pencil cases shaped like fire engines," she muttered.

Since the divorce, she realized, her orgasms were about as fulfilling as scratching an itch. Before Braden showed up on her lawn, there was no fantasizing, no scene setting... she would just crank on the vibe and knock one out in lieu of an Ambien. It was ludicrous that she'd lost her virginity twenty-three years ago, yet still had no idea what turned her on. *What was she, a fucking Puritan?*

The day passed in a blur of colorful school supplies and more colorful language.

As she pulled into her driveway after a long drive home from the studio, the rational part of her was relieved that Braden's truck wasn't there. She hadn't heard from him since their talk, and she couldn't imagine when she would be ready to face him again.

The evening was warm and her back yard looked welcoming thanks to all the work he had done. She decided to prune some of her flower bushes while attempting to get in touch with her inner sex kitten. After a quick dinner, she pulled on her cut-off shorts and a gauzy cotton tank top. At the last minute, she decided she would feel sexier if she removed her bra, letting the soft shirt skim directly across her skin. Voluptuous as she was, she hardly ever went braless outside of her bedroom, but this felt... nice. She grabbed a pair of clippers from the garage, then headed out back.

As she cut into an overgrown crepe myrtle, a breeze blew through the loose sides of her top. The fabric brushed deliciously against her peaked nipples, and she felt a surge of sexual awareness followed by a wave of self-loathing. She bagged her clippings and reflected on the root of that negativity.

Lisa had been self-conscious about her breasts on and off throughout her life. She'd had none to speak of until she was about fourteen, but she made up for lost time and filled out a C-cup by her junior year of high school. The larger breasts balanced her small waist and curvy bottom, and for a little while she had a lot of confidence and male attention.

Until Ricky Lavin. They had only dated for a few months when she was sixteen. It was a forgettable relationship in nearly every regard, but for a throw-away comment he made one night. Funny how painful memories remained the most vivid. She clipped another crepe myrtle, and let the past in.

They had been watching a scary movie with friends in someone's huge basement media room, and snuck off to take advantage of the darkness and lack of parental supervision. The shag carpet was itchy on her back, she remembered. They made out for a while and she let him unhook her bra -- the first boy who had been granted that privilege. As he played ineptly with her breasts (though it was years before she knew any better), he paused between kisses to say, "You need to firm these things up." His dad was a well-regarded gynecologist, so she had assumed Ricky knew what he was talking about.

Twenty-five years later, Lisa paused with hedge clippers in mid-air and shook her head. One asinine remark from a cocky high school kid, and she'd hated her breasts ever since. With the wisdom of hindsight and advanced age, it finally hit her: *there had been absolutely nothing wrong with her teenage breasts.* With a deep sigh, she longed to have her young body back.

She regretted the years of insecurity -- the clothes not worn, the sex not had. If Ricky hadn't been an ignorant little shit, if she hadn't taken his comment to heart, her life would've been so different. Maybe she would've flashed passing cars or entered a wet t-shirt contest after all, she chuckled to herself. Maybe she would've won.

The thought of that ignited something inside her. She pressed her thighs together because at that moment, her body demanded it. It was a similar sensation to what she felt when Braden admitted seeing her long-ago, accidental nipple-flash.

She bent to scoop clippings into a trash bag. The light evening breeze caressed the sides of her breasts and ribcage through the wide arm openings of her loose shirt. She shrugged to help the shirt slip a little further off her shoulder until one breast was hardly covered at all. She thought about how embarrassed she would be if anyone saw her like this. Just imagining it made her pussy clench.

"Oh-- Ms. Taylor. You're home." The voice came from behind her.

Lisa jumped, startled out of her reverie. "Braden. Hi."

"Sorry to--" he stared at her. "Jesus."

She resisted the urge to cross her arms. It had been years since she last felt sexy, and she wasn't about to let it go. "You've done such a great job with the rest of the yard; I couldn't let these bushes go any longer."

"Uh-huh." He absently patted the front of his shorts, drawing Lisa's attention to what appeared to be an impressive erection. She was mentally congratulating herself for causing it, when he reached into his front pocket and pulled out an eight-inch PVC pipe. "I mowed over a sprinkler the other day. It'll take me a minute to fix it."

"Thanks. I really do wish you'd let me give you something..." His eyes went black and she trailed off, as visions of sexual favors danced in their heads. Embarrassed by her unintentional double entendre, she lowered her eyes and realized the thick rod in his shorts had remained after he'd taken out the PVC. *God almighty.*

One corner of his mouth curled, and he indicated the pipe in his fist. "This'll only take a minute." His eyes flicked hotly over every inch of her, before he turned and found the broken pipe ten paces away.

Lisa forced herself not to watch him. It was nearly impossible, considering the way his old surf t-shirt clung to every slope and groove. Her panties got even wetter when she recalled the look on his face when he saw her. Obviously, being seen -- especially by him -- was a button-pusher. She rolled her eyes as she realized that she was a wannabe exhibitionist who hated her body. Natalie would love to trot out her minor in Psychology for that one.

She bent to pick up the clippers, aware of the sway of her unbound breasts as she moved. When she straightened to attack another bush, her shirt hung from the hard points of her nipples. She didn't have to look to know his eyes were on her. The feeling she got from that knowledge was a drug.

So what now, she wondered, as she clipped another bush. She couldn't very well go out in public, looking for age-appropriate men to flash. Well, she *could*, but she wasn't going to. For some reason, Braden liked to look at her. Why not show the grown boy what he wanted to see? Hell, he'd already seen more than he should have. What's the harm in showing him more of the same?

The harm would be to her ego when he realized he'd been fantasizing about 41 year-old breasts.

Lisa gave herself a mental shake and fervently hoped that wherever Ricky Lavin may be today, he was walking around with a huge set of floppy man-boobs.

Body image be damned.

She bent to bag the cuttings, knowing Braden would get a glimpse straight down her shirt if he was looking her way. Given his muttered curse, she assumed he was.

He came toward her radiating heat and restless energy. His voice was deeper than usual as he walked past saying, "I need to test the system. You'll wanna stand clear."

She watched him disappear behind the house to find the switch box.

And then she made a choice.

The sprinklers came on. Braden walked back around to find that Lisa hadn't budged. She'd only gotten drenched. He quickly shut off the system and jogged over to her.

Her skin was shiny and wet, and her waterlogged cut-offs dripped down her legs. The tissue-thin tank top was soaked, rosy-brown nipples protesting the cold.

She wrung out her hair and blinked spiky eyelashes at him. "Oops."

"Sorry, Ms. Taylor, I didn't mean to--" Then he seemed to realize she wasn't complaining. "*Fuck.*"

The heat in his eyes only made her shiver more. She hugged herself. He took a step closer, gently uncrossed her arms and set her hands at her sides. "Now, that is a gorgeous view."

It occurred to Lisa that she hadn't really thought this out.

Braden's eyes darted from her breasts to her face, with equal interest. His warm, rough hands slid from her wrists to her shoulders, up the sides of her neck and into her hair. He licked his lips and slowly pulled her close. She held her breath as he brushed that beautiful mouth against hers once... and again...

Then his hot tongue licked the seam of her lips, and Lisa willed herself to back away. "I'm sorry, Braden. I can't."

"You mean you won't." He sounded hurt and more than a little frustrated.

"I can't. So I won't." She crossed her arms to cover herself, rubbing her biceps against the sudden chill. "I'm forty-one years old."

"Yeah. And you're playing games like a high school girl." He pushed her arms down again, using light force when she resisted. Looking more angry than hurt, now, he held her in place with her wrists behind her back. "What, you think you're not attractive to men anymore? Is that it?"

Eyes wide, she didn't speak or even nod. She didn't have to.

A muscle in his jaw ticked in frustration. "Well, *Lisa*, in case you haven't noticed, I'm a man, and this is what you do to me."

With that, he kissed her roughly and ground his erection against her hard enough to hurt.

To the surprise of them both, she kissed him back just as roughly, biting his plush lower lip and sucking his tongue. He groaned and maneuvered them to a lounge chair, pulling her down on top of him. His smooth skin smelled of that woodsy soap and he tasted like spicy cinnamon. She wanted this. She needed this. She fucking *deserved* this.

But when she felt his hands lift the wet hem of her shirt, she panicked and shook her head, panting, "I'm not ready." Before his expression closed, she confessed, "I've been with no one besides Vance since I was younger than you." She saw him try to hide his surprise that she'd been celibate these last few years.

He sighed and brushed a damp curl off her cheek. "I didn't know." He kissed her forehead and let go of her. "I've waited half my life for you. I can wait a little longer."

"Thank you." She smiled gratefully and lightly kissed his mouth, then scooted back to sit between his calves, straddling his legs and the chair. Her nipples responded when his eyes grazed them, still very visible in the damp shirt. Aware of his hard-on and recalling horror stories about painful blue balls, she moved to cover herself, "Sorry--"

He shook his head. "Don't. I'll be glad to have real pictures in my head instead of my imagination when I go home to take care of this," he squeezed the thick bulge in his shorts. "Unless you wanna lend me a sock," he chuckled, all dimples and twinkling eyes.

Having his eyes on her was a turn-on. Knowing she got him hard, even more so. But seeing his hand with the braided leather cord around his thick wrist, long fingers delineating his straining erection...

"I could lend you a sock," she purred with an impish smile.

Understanding dawned in his eyes. "You really are trying to kill me," he said. Then he watched her face as he slowly slid his hand under his waistband.

Lisa had never been so turned-on in her life. Seeing the movement of Braden's hand as he worked his cock inside his shorts, while his heavy gaze alternated between her face and her tits... She'd have pressed her thighs together if she weren't straddling the chair. Luckily, her shorts were still wet, else her condition would be all too evident. The flexing muscles of his forearm fascinated her. In her struggle to keep her restless hands off of him, she ran them over her breasts, squirming against his legs when her fingers caught on hardened nipples.

He made a sound like a growl. "Show me, Lisa. Let me see you."

She was terrified, but she trusted him. Inch by inch, she lifted the hem of her shirt until the fabric brushed up and over her nipples and her breasts were fully revealed to his hungry eyes.

"You're perfect," he ground out. "Still. Perfect." The fist in his shorts worked faster. He lifted his free hand, surprising her when, instead of reaching for her breasts, he laced his fingers with hers. Despite his obsession with her assets, he stared into her eyes when his hand tightened on hers, pulsed a few times, then relaxed.

His eyes drifted closed as he caught his breath, chest heaving, lips flushed, a glimpse of hard, tanned belly where his shirt hiked up when he'd pulled his hand out of his shorts.

He was the most beautiful thing Lisa had ever seen.

Chapter Eight

LISA TUGGED THE cold, damp shirt back down to cover her breasts. The heat of embarrassment washed over her, along with the incongruous side-effect she had come to anticipate. Her nipples ached, they were so hard.

Braden opened his eyes, and his look shot straight to her core. "What about you?"

"I'm fine."

"Is that an, 'I was unmoved by the whole experience,' fine, or an 'I'll take care of myself the second you leave,' fine?"

"I promised you a sock, didn't I?" She started to stand, but it was tricky as her legs still straddled his.

In one fluid motion, he untangled their legs and pinned hers under his. "Little late for that," he chuckled, tugging at his shorts.

"Sorry. Guess I got distracted," she said, trying for glib.

He put his warm hands on her legs, lightly stroking the sensitive skin behind her knees. "I can think of better ways to distract you." His hands skimmed up her thighs until his fingertips disappeared into her shorts and short-circuited her central nervous system.

"I have no doubt," she set her hands on top of his, holding him in place. "But that's about as much distraction as I can handle for one day." To her great relief, he understood and didn't try to push her for more.

Dressed as she was -- or wasn't -- she couldn't walk him all the way to his truck, so they said goodbye in the shadows on the side of the house. She hugged him, forcing herself not to press her face against his chest. "Thank you, Braden."

"The pleasure was all mine," he said with a rueful smile. Then he kissed the corner of her lips, and made sure to catch her eye so there was no mistaking his meaning when he added, *"I'll see you again, soon, Lisa."*

The moment she heard his truck drive away, she rushed inside, stripped off her wet clothes and brought herself to an explosive orgasm. Just as they both knew she would.

* * *

She took a ticket and pulled into the law office lot. Parking her eight year-old Honda between two sleek European sports cars, she thought about mid-life crises. Maybe she was having one. Too bad hers didn't include a hot new car.

Her cameras and other equipment made the walk across the parking lot difficult. She had to press the handicap access button with her foot to open the door to the building. A young woman who looked to be somebody's slutty secretary sneered as she walked by. Lisa knew she looked ridiculous carrying all her gear, but there was no room in her tight budget for decent wheeled cases.

As she struggled to get everything clear of the elevator doors before they closed, a silver-haired man was kind enough to hold the "open" button and ask for her floor. "Looks like we're going to the same place," he said.

She smiled politely and adjusted her gear so it cut into a different spot on her shoulder.

"You must be the photographer." He was in his mid-40s, Lisa figured, and classically handsome, like Cary Grant or another of those old clean-cut Hollywood actors her grandma used to get all dreamy about.

"What was your first clue?" She chuckled.

"The cameras tipped me off," he shrugged a pin-striped shoulder. "But I'm sleuthy like that."

She smiled. "I'm Lisa Taylor. I'd shake your hand, but..."

"Your hands are full. I'm Thomas Porter, senior partner."

"Then I'll be shooting you today."

"With a camera, I hope," he said with a grin female jurors probably found charming. The car stopped and he held the doors open for her. "We've reserved a conference room for your use. It's right this way."

Lisa found it strange and a little rude that he didn't offer to help carry her things. Of course, he was a lawyer -- maybe he was simply being cautious, thinking about liability if any of her expensive equipment were to be damaged.

Walking behind the handsome, successful and age-appropriate man, she noticed he didn't wear a wedding ring. She checked out the rest of him because she felt she should, but there was no telling what kind of body he did or didn't have under all that custom tailored gray wool. Comparisons to Braden were inevitable, but she needed to push all thoughts of him out of her mind and focus on the work.

They arrived at the designated conference room, and she set down her gear with relief. "This is perfect, thank you."

"My pleasure. I'll see you soon, Lisa." He nodded with a small smile and walked away.

Christ. Fantastic choice of words. She sucked in a deep breath as her last moments with Braden came rushing back, muddling her mind and dampening her panties.

Did she just need to get laid, or did she specifically need *him*? She made herself save that riddle for later, so she could think about what she was doing while setting up the backdrop and lighting. Between having her rates cut on catalogue work, and the bills that were getting the best of her, this job was too important to fuck up.

There were twelve partners at Chandler & Simmons, P.A., the law firm Natalie's father had co-founded. Lisa had met Mr. Simmons a couple times and thought he was kind of a jerk, but that was probably due to the tremendous stick up his ass. It annoyed Lisa to no end that Natalie worked so hard and was the smartest person Lisa knew, but they hadn't made her a partner, yet. Even worse was the way Natalie's dad dangled her potential partnership like a carrot, and she kept pushing harder and harder to reach it.

Mr. Simmons' executive assistant had done her best to schedule the partners' photography sessions around their various meetings and court appearances. With twelve sittings, it would've been a long day even if nobody's schedule changed, but of course there were glitches. Lisa was able to stay focused while working with each of the partners. She had to be fully present in the moment to get the lighting just right, and to coax natural smiles out of some flat personalities and busy curmudgeons. Between sittings, though, sometimes she had to wait a while. At those times, it was nearly impossible to keep Braden out of her head.

When Natalie joined her in the conference room for a quick lunch, Lisa asked about the partners she'd photographed and those she had yet to meet. This strategy worked to keep the conversation off the topic of Braden, as well as to provide some interesting backstory and a few laughs.

"Who's coming in next?"

Lisa checked her list. "Margaret Byington, then Thomas Porter. Oh yeah, he's the one I met in the elevator."

Natalie double-checked that the door was closed, then leaned in. "Thomas is the office hottie. The support staff swoons en masse when he walks by."

"He's nice-looking, but 'hottie' seems a little extreme," Lisa laughed.

"Compared to the rest of the yahoos around here?"

Lisa conceded the point with a grin and a nod. "What's his story? I think he was flirting with me this morning."

"I'm sure he was. As of about six months ago, he's single again. Again."

"Huh?"

"His second marriage lasted like a year and a half. The wife was a shrew. But he's a decent guy, has a few kids with wife number one." Natalie studied her. "So... if he was flirting, would you be interested?"

"I dunno. Maybe. I think I ought to be," she shrugged.

A short while later, Lisa easily moved men to the back of her mind, as photographing Margaret Byington required her absolute, complete attention. The woman couldn't have been more than forty, but she dressed like a schoolmarm and carried herself like an octogenarian. Actually, Lisa's grandmother had more life in her at age ninety than the stodgy Ms. Byington. If this was the kind of woman who made partner at Chandler & Simmons, P.A., it was no wonder Natalie was still only an associate.

"If you could tip your chin a little to your left... good. Right there. Now smile..."

"This is a professional portrait. I wouldn't want to look glib."

"You won't look glib. I promise." Lisa's camera whirred as she finally coaxed a lukewarm smile out of Ms. Byington. The woman looked like she should smell of moth balls, but at least her portrait wouldn't do the same.

Between sittings, her phone buzzed with a text from Braden. *RU home? I just picked up a new air filter.*

She responded: *You're so sweet, but I'm on an all-day shoot...*

Do you still keep that key under the flower pot?

Shit. Was there anything embarrassing lying around? She hadn't left her vibrator on the nightstand, had she? No, she was sure it was in the drawer. She tapped out: *Yes, but you don't have to make a special trip for that!*

I live around the corner, remember? I'll go take care of it.

Thanks so much!!!

My pleasure, Lisa. ;-)

His texted wink made her stomach flip as if it were the real thing. Jesus. Nat was right; she really did need to get out more.

She tucked the phone away right as Thomas Porter leaned in with his perfect head of silver hair and his straight, white smile. "Are you ready for me?"

"I sure am." If he noticed her flushed cheeks, she hoped he was over-confident enough to assume he had caused them. "C'mon in and take the hot seat."

As expected, he was an easy subject to photograph. He knew, either by instinct or practice, which was his good side and how to angle his shoulders. His blue-gray eyes squinted just the right amount to warm his "trust me" smile.

"That'll do it." She stepped back from her camera and grinned, "You've done this before, haven't you?"

"Guilty." He chuckled and stood. "You know, Lisa, Natalie showed me your portfolio, and I must say I was impressed by your work. I plan to order a few prints for my office."

"Thank you, Mr. Porter."

"It's Thomas. And I'd like to take you to dinner sometime."

She smiled. "I'd like that, too." What's not to like? He was handsome and charming, and she wouldn't be mortified if anyone saw them together. They would probably have a good time, and she was sure kissing him would be... nice.

When she finally got home that evening, it was after seven. Thoughts of Thomas evaporated as she wandered down the hall to the air vent, expecting to feel some remnant of Braden's having been there earlier. There was a small fluff of lint on the floor, but the lingering scent of woodsy soap was only in her head.

She looked around as if she were Braden, alone in her house. Did he simply come in through the kitchen, make a beeline for the air vent, swap the new filter for the old, and then go back out the way he came? Or was he curious enough to explore a little? Before he left, did he set the old filter on the floor, then go in search of her bedroom? Would he have stood in the doorway or boldly entered? She didn't think he'd be so disrespectful as to look in her drawers, but would he have sniffed the perfume on her dresser, or perused the books on her nightstand? Was her bedspread still smooth from when she made it that morning, or had Braden rumpled it that afternoon then smoothed it out again before he left?

As she heated some soup for dinner, she tried to think about what it would be like to date Thomas, but her stubborn mind kept jumping back to Braden. She couldn't help imagining him in her room when she wasn't home... lying on her bed, sliding his hand under his waistband...

It turned her on to think about it.

<u>Chapter Nine</u>

AS SHE GOT ready for bed that night, Lisa didn't bother to put on a night shirt. She was so achy with need, there was no question she would be strumming herself to sleep. The cool sheets felt wonderful on her hot skin. *Had she really not slept nude since her honeymoon with Vance? Why the hell not?*

She closed her eyes and brushed her fingers across her cheek, over her lips, remembering Braden's kiss. Skimming her hands over her breasts, she pretended he was touching her. From her swollen breasts to her pulsing clit, her entire body responded more to the Braden of her imagination than it ever had to Vance. Or anyone else, for that matter. But she was too busy to think about that right now.

As if he were reading her mind, her phone buzzed with a text. *Hi.*
She pressed her thighs together and responded: *Hi.*

I want to come over.

His words echoed in her head while the angel and devil on her shoulders battled it out. The angel won, barely: *It's late. I'm in bed.*

Even better. ;-) Did I wake you?

No.

Did I... interrupt you?

Lisa sucked in a breath. What the hell? Did he plant a spy cam in her room when he was there earlier? While she debated the intelligence of an honest reply, the devil on her shoulder replied: *Yes.*

Do you mind?

No.

He didn't respond for a minute, but then her phone pinged his request for video chat. Her heart pounded as she stared at it. Before she could change her mind, she rejected the request.

Her pussy clenched when he texted: *We're doing the same thing, Lisa.*

Then he added: *I'm already thinking about you, but this would be much more interesting if we could see each other.*

The devil on her shoulder strangled the angel and tossed her into oblivion.

Lisa heard herself make a little sound of longing as she tapped out: *Ok.*

This time, when he requested a video chat, she tugged the sheet up over her breasts, positioned the phone on the nightstand, and accepted.

"Hi again," he said with the sexiest grin ever. He was lying on his left side, propped on his elbow. He wasn't wearing a shirt, but Lisa could only see about halfway down his abs. That was a relief, as she wasn't prepared to see all of him just yet. It was enough that his right bicep was flexing in a slow rhythm that hinted at what the rest of that arm was doing off-screen.

"Hi again." Her phone slipped and she repositioned it against the lamp. "Sorry. I don't have a stand and my lighting sucks."

"You look beautiful. What little I can see of you, anyway."

Her fist had a white-knuckled grip on the sheet above her breasts. "This will probably not come as a surprise, but I've never done this before."

"You've never masturbated?"

She chuckled. "No, I've done that."

His pupils overtook his blue-green irises. "No one else has ever watched you?"

"No one else has ever asked." She took a deep breath and let go of the sheet. It caught on her hardened nipples, then slid to her waist.

"God, you're gorgeous." With the way his voice caught in his throat when he said that, she could almost believe it. She watched his reaction as she palmed her breasts, pushed them up and together, teased and pinched her nipples.

His right bicep tightened and held a moment. "Put your hand in your panties," he rasped.

"I'm not wearing any."

"*Fuck*. Touch your pussy for me. Please."

She held his eyes and skimmed her hand down her belly and beneath the sheet. Her soft moan told him when her fingers had arrived.

He licked his lips. "Tell me how it feels."

This was all so far out of her comfort zone, she may as well have been attending via satellite. "It feels good," she attempted.

"You can do better than that," he chided.

"Jesus," she gasped, and slid her fingers over and around her clit. "Hot. Swollen. Wet. I'm fucking drenched."

His face tightened and his bicep stilled once more. "Show me."

Her fingers stopped. "Why can't this be enough?"

"Because I want to see how you touch yourself, so we can both imagine my tongue on you."

The words nearly took her over the edge. She pushed the sheet away and slid across the bed, letting him see every inch of her. His eyes followed her middle finger as it disappeared between puffy pink lips, then came back glistening to tease her engorged clit.

"Braden." It was only a whisper, but it got his attention. "Let me see you."

His brows furrowed. "*God, Lisa*," he ground out as he briefly disappeared from view. Then she saw him. All of him. The beautiful face. The hard chest. The ridged abs and the V-cuts. One muscular arm bent behind his head, the other extended down to where his hand moved slowly from root to tip of a penis as perfectly-sculpted as the rest of him.

Lisa strummed with more purpose. Her other hand skimmed over her breasts, teasing one hard nipple, then the other. Braden watched her intently, his fist matching tempo with her fingers. The head of his cock was flushed and swollen, and Lisa licked her lips, wishing it was disappearing into her mouth, rather than his hand.

At the thought, she ground her impossibly-hard clit against her palm, and moaned a loud, wet release. A heartbeat later, Braden's fist tightened as thick ropes of semen shot onto his chest.

* * *

Lisa spent the next day on a sickening roller-coaster of adrenaline spikes and morning-after regrets. The regrets hit the moment her eyes popped open. The adrenaline began when she heard the message she had missed while berating herself in the shower, "Mrs. Taylor, this is Paul at Camp Big League, again. Your check still hasn't cleared, and as you know full payment is required for Jake to finish the summer here..."

Thoughts of Jake coming home led directly to Braden and the stupid, *stupid* thing she did last night. Obviously, it would never happen again. She'd swear Braden to secrecy and pray to all that is holy that no one else -- especially Vance, Elena and above all, Jake -- ever found out.

Which brought on another surge of adrenaline, since it was fucking Vance's fault that her fucking check didn't clear. But he was on fucking vacation in fucking Europe with fucking Elena, and couldn't be bothered to respond to Lisa's fucking messages.

Of course, if Vance and Elena weren't in Europe, Braden wouldn't have had the house to himself, so he wouldn't have had enough privacy for video chat, and Lisa wouldn't now be plagued with self-loathing.

And so it went.

She dodged Braden's calls and texts, using the true excuse that she was busy editing the portrait shots of the lawyers. (It really wasn't easy making the stone-faced look life-like.) She swapped email with Jake, keeping it light and not letting on that he might soon be kicked out of his favorite place in the world, or that she had let his oldest friend and childhood hero watch her masturbate while he did the same. Mother of the fucking year, she was.

By the end of the week, the mood swings had her feeling schizophrenic. When she stopped by the law firm to drop off the portrait proofs, she didn't try to avoid Natalie's intuitive grilling. She *needed* it, knowing her friend wouldn't judge her for being such a huge freaking idiot. But Mr. Simmons was dangling the partnership carrot again, so Nat hardly looked up from her work when Lisa came by. She'd hoped to see Thomas while she was there -- since she looked like shit and felt even worse, it would've been easy to make an excuse to cancel their date the following night. Unfortunately, he wasn't around.

Checking email before bed that night, she broke into hysterical laughter when her catalogue client officially cut her fees again. It was just the cherry on top of her crappy life.

When Thomas called Saturday afternoon to confirm their date, Lisa couldn't bring herself to cancel. There were worse ways to spend a few hours than having a nice dinner in the company of an attractive, intelligent man, so she dragged herself out of bed and into the shower.

She owned a few cocktail dresses, but it had been years since she'd had occasion to wear them. The little black dress she had worn to Vance's company's holiday gala; the sleek red dress she had worn to Vance's fortieth birthday party; and the blush-colored knit she had worn to Braden's sister's wedding. Despite a lengthy battle with various undergarments of torture, the blush was the only dress that fit well enough to wear in public.

It wasn't her first choice for tonight, but it was a pretty dress. The rich, nude color complemented her skin tone. The deep square neckline showed more cleavage than she was usually comfortable with, but the knee-skimming skirt flared just enough to hide the round hips and ass she had inherited from her grandmother. With high-heeled black pumps, the ensemble accentuated the positive and eliminated the negative as well as she could hope.

After styling her hair to fall in soft golden waves around her shoulders, she applied minimal makeup. Luckily, she had also inherited her grandmother's skin, so she only needed a little powder foundation, although she added a sweep of blush because she looked sallow. Her dark-chocolate eyes (her best feature, if she had to choose something) needed no more enhancement than a few strokes of mascara. She slicked on sheer berry lipstick and stepped through a cloud of jasmine perfume, right as the doorbell rang at ten minutes to seven.

Pasting on a smile, she opened the door. "Hi, you're early--" Her arm itched with the urge to slam the door when she saw Braden on the other side.

He looked her up and down with appreciation. "Looks to me like I'm right on time."

"Sorry. Didn't realize it was you." She couldn't look him in the eye, so she stepped outside and made a production of locking the door and putting her keys in her bag.

"Yeah, I got that."

"I was on my way out."

"Got that, too." He moved aside to let her pass and followed her down the steps to the driveway. "Nice dress."

"It's old," she shrugged. "I wore it to Stephanie's wedding."

"I remember. It still looks amazing on you."

She knew she was being a bitch and he didn't deserve that. "Thanks." She risked a glance at his face. There was hurt in his eyes and anger tightened his jaw.

"So you hate me now." It was a statement of fact.

"I don't hate you," she said to her shoes.

"So much for not bullshitting each other. I knew you weren't editing all week."

"Actually, I was."

He toyed with a lock of her hair, fingers brushing her bare shoulder. "Then why won't you look at me?"

"Because I've seen too much of you already." She stepped out of reach. "That shouldn't have happened."

"Why the hell not?" Before Lisa could answer, one of the sleek European sports cars from the law firm parking lot pulled up. As Thomas emerged from the expensive convertible, Braden chuckled without humor and muttered, "Fucking classic."

Thomas came around the car with a charming smile for Lisa. "You look beautiful," he said, kissing the air near her ear.

Braden cleared his throat. "G'night, Ms. Taylor. I'll be by tomorrow to mow the lawn."

As he turned away, Thomas said, "Wait. You look familiar. Have we met?"

"I don't believe so, sir," Braden said with such excessive deference, Lisa half-expected him to touch his forelock.

"Thomas Porter, this is Braden Healey." With her eyes, Lisa begged Braden to behave. "Braden's an old family friend. He's been helping out around here while my son's at camp."

"Yes!" Thomas shook Braden's hand enthusiastically. "Of course, Brady Healey! Great to meet you. I'm a fan. You went to high school with my daughter and I followed your college career. Your injury was the shits." Lisa winced at his failed attempt to seem cool.

"Yeah, it was, but thanks," Braden said graciously. "Who's your daughter?"

"Olivia Porter. She was a cheerleader and you had some classes together over the years."

Lisa was sure Braden glanced at her with a mischievous glint in his eye before responding, "Olivia, yeah. Sweet girl. Pretty, too, if you won't hit me for saying so."

"Not at all," Thomas laughed. "Hey, she's home for the summer and she's not dating anyone. You should give her a call."

"Good idea." Braden looked at Lisa, and she hoped he didn't see her clenching her jaw.

Thomas suddenly remembered why he was there. "Guess we should get going or we'll lose our reservation." He opened the car door for Lisa and jogged around to slide behind the wheel. "Great to meet you, Brady."

"You too, Mr. Porter." As soon as Lisa had lowered herself into the deep seat and pulled her legs in, Braden pushed her door shut. She tugged her skirt down when she saw him eyeing the shadow between her thighs. Thomas revved the engine and Braden winked at her. "You kids have fun," he grinned.

<u>Chapter Ten</u>

LISA COULDN'T HAVE known that the date she accepted to get her mind off Braden would consist mostly of conversation *about* Braden.

Thomas wasn't kidding when he said he was a fan. Apparently, Braden had been the star of Thomas's college fantasy football team for four years, until the shoulder injury. Sometime during dessert, the conversation turned to their kids. Thomas handed her his phone and she was treated to dozens of pictures of Olivia, with her blonde hair, blue eyes, and perky everything.

When they got back to her house, Thomas realized, "I'm sorry. I talked about football all night, didn't I?"

"It's fine. I didn't mind." Was he looking at her strangely? All evening, Lisa had been certain her face was an open book whenever Braden's name was mentioned. An open *picture* book, depicting every sick thing she'd done or thought about doing. The paranoia had her delicious dinner sitting like lead in her belly.

"Okay. Good." He walked her to the door. "I had a nice time tonight."

"Yes, so did I," she lied and kissed him on the cheek. "Thank you, Thomas." She unlocked the door and they stood in awkward silence while she pretended not to know he was hoping she would invite him in. It was only nine-thirty, but she mustered up a yawn and he got the hint.

When she was finally alone, she dropped the dress on her bedroom floor and turned the shower on scalding. She had to try to scrub off the guilt and self-loathing. The memory flashed of Braden staring at the shadow between her thighs as he closed the car door. Dozens of similar flashes followed and she felt the familiar quickening in her core. *What was wrong with her?* With purpose, she stepped under the painfully-hot water. She refused to relieve the needy ache. God, she was stupid! She had no business even thinking of Braden. Her head filled with images of Vance sneering, Elena yelling, and Jake looking angry and hurt.

By the time she felt clean again, her skin glowed pink from scrubbing. The hot shower had dehydrated her, so she wrapped herself in a thick towel, combed her wet hair down her back, and walked out in a cloud of steam.

The kitchen windows were black with night as she drank a glass of cold water. Hours later, she would wonder why she wasn't startled when the motion-sensing back porch light came on. She intended to ignore Braden's light knock, but he saw her through the sidelight window. His mouth was tight, his face was serious with intent, and his hair looked to have been repeatedly tousled by frustrated hands.

"Open the door, Lisa."

She shook her head. "No. It's late and I'm not dressed."

"Open the door."

"Whatever it is can wait 'til tomorrow."

"No, it can't." He held her eyes as he bent to retrieve the key from under the flower pot.

She backed away from the door. "Fine. Okay. Put the key back, I'll be right out..."

But he had already let himself in.

She took another step back. "Listen, I'm sorry I let it go so far. It was wrong."

He pushed the door closed and stalked toward her.

"It was *all* wrong," she continued and backed up a few more steps. "I should've said no before. I'm saying it now."

He kept moving closer, eyes dark with intent. "I'm not asking now."

Lisa's mouth went dry. Acutely aware of how close to naked she was, she held her towel in place with both hands and backed away until her ass hit the cabinet. She felt her heart pounding between her legs.

"Seriously, Braden. Get out or I'll call the police."

He pressed his phone into her hand. "You'll need this, then."

In the span of a heartbeat, he effortlessly lifted her onto the counter, pushed her knees apart and covered her pussy with his hot, beautiful mouth. The phone slid out of her hand and skittered down the counter, out of reach. She intended to push him away, but somehow her fingers tangled in his thick, sandy hair, pulling him closer instead. His hum of approval vibrated against her.

Her face heated with embarrassment when he sat back on his heels and took in the view. The rest of her heated with something else when he brushed the pad of his thumb across her swollen pink wetness. She tried to close her legs, but his big hands opened her wider. He leaned in and gave her a long, flat-tongued lick, then teased her with tiny feathery kisses, everywhere but where she needed him most.

"Please."

"Please what?" He kissed her inner thigh. "Should I stop?"

"Yes, but please don't," she begged.

"That was rhetorical." He bit the inside of her other thigh. "I've wanted you like this for too long to stop now," he murmured at her center, warm breath taunting her sensitive skin. He swirled his tongue in her entrance, lapping at her wetness. Then he licked her smooth outer labia, one side then the other, holding her still so she couldn't push herself into his mouth. Her cunt was so swollen, it felt inside-out.

Finally, his plush lips found her clit, nibbling lightly, coaxing it to a level of arousal she had never felt before. She thought she might happily die when he pressed it between his lips and gave her a soft sweep of his tongue. He surprised her with a gentle scrape of teeth, then sucked her hard little organ into his mouth and lashed it with his tongue until she shattered in technicolor shards.

"So damn sweet. I knew you would be." He licked his lips and kissed her. She hesitated a moment; her scent was on his face, her taste on his tongue. And for the first time ever, she was good with that.

"More." She deepened the kiss and let her hands roam over his soft t-shirt, exploring the hard muscle underneath. Her nails skimmed the tight points of his nipples, eliciting a groan from him. He scooped her off the counter and she wrapped her legs around his waist, grinding her wet heat into him when she felt his erection.

Somehow Lisa's towel was still in place when he set her on her feet in the bedroom. Thankful she'd left on a small lamp rather than the unforgiving ceiling light, she was about to open the towel when Braden stopped her. "Let me."

He sat on the edge of the bed in front of her, holding her eyes as he tugged the towel open and let it fall. With an almost innocent reverence, he slid his hands up her ribcage and cupped her breasts. His hands were warm, calloused palms teasing her hardened peaks. Lisa fingered the worn leather braid around his wrist in an attempt to convince herself this was really happening.

Rasping his tongue across her left nipple, he whispered, "Finally," and pulled it deep into his mouth, sucking hard. The breathtaking tug shot straight to her core. She felt herself bloom as his lips and tongue worked one nipple then the other.

"Braden... stop."

He jerked away, stricken, lips rosy and wet from suckling her. She gripped the hem of his t-shirt and lifted it, revealing his lean, muscled stomach. With a relieved chuckle, he reached behind his head and yanked the shirt off.

"Christ, you had me worried there for a second." He pulled her onto his lap and kissed her, hands exploring her curvy bottom.

Devouring his mouth, she savored his spicy taste and the brush of his bare chest against hers. She pressed him back on the bed, straddling his thighs. From a distance, his skin looked so smooth she had assumed he waxed his chest, but now she fingered the soft dusting of golden down.

With a fingertip, she traced the definition of his pectorals, along the deep ridges between his abs. In response, his fingers tightened their grip on her ass. He inhaled sharply when she licked and bit his nipples, groaned when she pressed wet, sucking kisses down his stomach. She dipped her tongue under the waistband of his jeans, and licked the tip of his cock as it strained to get out.

"You're overdressed," she admonished.

He slipped out from under her and seconds later stood fully nude and impossibly beautiful. Pulling her up, he grabbed her neck and kissed her deeply, his heavy erection hot against her belly.

Lisa bit his lips, breaking the kiss. She kissed the little white scar on his chin and nuzzled his neck, drunk on the fragrant cocktail of woodsy soap and aroused male. Planting moist kisses over the slope of his chest and down his ridged belly, she watched his eyes grow darker and more hooded the further south she traveled. As she sank to her knees, his cock bobbed toward her breasts. She wrapped one hand around his thick base and gently palmed his tight balls with the other. Never breaking eye contact, she ran her tongue up his length, curling it around his crown and licking a drop of pre-cum, before taking him fully into her mouth.

"Lisa. *Jesus,*" he bit out, fisting a hand in her hair.

She sucked him deep then released him slowly, inch by inch, covering his smooth velvet head with swirling licks before swallowing him again. Stroking the shaft in her hand, she was amazed how hard he was. She never knew a penis could *get* that hard.

Much as she loved having him in her mouth, she released him with a little wet *pop* panting, "In me."

"Fuck. Yes." He kissed her hard and retrieved a condom from his discarded pants.

Lisa sat back against the pillows and watched him sheath himself. He crawled up the bed, pausing along the way to push her thighs open, suckle her clit, and fuck her with his tongue. When they were face to face again, he licked at her mouth and teased her slick entrance with his cock. She bucked her hips in a desperate attempt to capture him.

"Now. Braden, now."

"*Yes.*" He slammed in to the hilt, stretching her. Their mouths fused in a ravenous kiss while he pulled out slowly... achingly slowly. Her pussy tightened around him. He squeezed her swollen breasts, catching their tight tips between his fingers, then rammed home again.

"God!" It seemed impossible, but Lisa would've sworn he was even harder than moments before. She raked her nails down his back and dug them into his tight, round ass as he withdrew once more. He bit and sucked the sensitive juncture of her neck and shoulder, then flexed his hips and nailed her. *Hard.* Her walls quivered around him. She'd never had an orgasm during intercourse before, but that was about to change -- he was hitting places deep inside her no one else had ever touched.

Braden made a sound of pleasure deep in his throat. "If I'd had any idea ten years ago that you'd feel this good, I would've jacked off even more."

Her breathless chuckle became a gasp when he slipped a hand between them and captured her clit in a firm pinch. She heard herself shout as she climaxed, and her pussy sucked him in, milking him, until he pulsed with his own forceful release.

Lisa blinked back to earth, only vaguely aware when Braden briefly rolled away to dispose of the condom. He pulled her back against his chest and kissed her shoulder, holding her close while their breathing returned to normal.

The voices in her head clamored for their turn at the mike. All concerns about Vance and Elena got an immediate boot, because fuck them. She reasoned with the "What about Jake" minstrel, pointing out that her son was fifteen, and her sex life was simply none of his business. That left her to contend with the "Yo Chubby" chanters and the "Really, Cougar, Could You Be Any More Cliche?" harpies. And they were some tenacious bitches.

She felt the dread creep in. Any thought of moving on with life from right this minute was fraught with embarrassment.

Should I say something?

How does my stomach look at this angle? Can I sneak away to grab a bathrobe?

He's really quiet.

What if he falls asleep? Should I let him stay?

This was just a one-time thing, right? What if he wants more than that?

What if he doesn't?

Before her thought spiral could get totally out of control, she felt an unmistakable nudge at her behind. Incredulous, she blurted, "You're still hard?"

"Not 'still,' but I'm hard again, yeah." There was a lazy smile in his voice.

She felt him flex against her. "My god."

"You did this to me."

Rolling over, she eyed his impressive hard-on. "You're twenty-three. A good sneeze would do that to you."

"I'll cop to a decent recovery time," he grinned, trailing a fingertip across the tops of her breasts. "But no one else has ever made me so hard I could break a fucking cinderblock with my dick."

"Flattery will get you everywhere," she chuckled, stroking him.

"Hey." He stilled her hand and waited for her to meet his eyes. When she did, he was scowling. "That wasn't flattery. It was honesty."

"Oh." It didn't compute. None of it.

"I swear, somehow, I'm gonna make you see yourself the way I see you." He licked and bit one nipple, then the other. "But first, I'm gonna make you scream again."

<u>**Chapter Eleven**</u>

"IT WON'T PROVE anything.   I'm not going grocery shopping braless."

Lisa had been relieved when Braden left of his own accord the night before, but she gave him an earful when he woke her up early this morning. He had called with a ridiculous proposition, the result of which found them sitting here in his truck on the far side of a Kroger parking lot in Duluth.

"Deal's a deal," he shrugged.

"But it's freezing in there!"

"Is it?" he asked with phony innocence.

A flash of humiliation sent a charge to her clit. The fact that she was getting turned on by this was more embarrassing than the public indecency.   "Pick something else. You can't possibly understand how naked I feel when the girls are loose. I don't even go braless in my house!"

"You went braless in your back yard."

"Only because I didn't expect to see anyone!" He laughed at her and she glared back.   "If I do this, you swear you'll retake the MCAT?"

"Yep." They had a staring contest, which Lisa promptly lost.

She sighed and reached back under her pale pink t-shirt for her bra hooks, then paused. "And soon. Not like a year from now or something."

"Soon. Like a month." He watched through lowered lashes as she unhooked her bra, slipped an arm through a strap, and pulled the whole thing out the other sleeve.

She dropped the bra in his lap and tugged her shirt back in place. "And you'll study this time."

"I will study this time." He fingered the smooth pink satin, enjoying the texture.

"And apply to med schools after."

"You're asking an awful lot for one little trip to Kroger," he said. "Applications... that's another negotiation entirely."

She frowned at him, but opted not to debate it yet. Her heart was pounding and her nipples were already tight with anticipation. "Let's just get this over with."

As planned, Braden walked in first and loitered near a seasonal beer display. Lisa took a cart and headed toward the produce section, knowing he would casually follow. It occurred to her that "horny and ridiculous" was a strange mix of emotions. She avoided eye contact with other shoppers and crossed her arms near a mother with young kids. When she stopped to bag some apples, her phone buzzed with a text. *Banana guy is staring.*

She risked a glance and saw a nerdy middle-aged man who seemed very concerned with choosing the right bunch of bananas. She responded: *Yeah. At bananas.*

You almost caught him but he was watching YOU beautiful. Then he added, *Go get some popsicles.*

I don't need popsicles.

He grinned as her phone buzzed. *I'm in the mood for something cold.*

Lisa gave him the evil eye and turned down the freezer aisle. She found the popsicles and opened the freezer door to take a box. The blast of icy air took her breath away and made her nipples strain against the fitted shirt. She walked past Braden, pretending not to know him. Pretending not to feel his stare or to hear him curse under his breath.

As she looked at fresh bread in the bakery, he texted: *Stock boy piled bagels on top of donuts. LOL he has no idea. You're so hot he can't stop looking at you.*

She rolled her eyes. *Of course people are looking at me! I've got big tits jiggling around a grocery store without a bra!*

She heard him chuckle as she chose a loaf of sourdough bread and added it to her cart.

"Finding everything okay, ma'am?" The store manager appeared beside her. At least she assumed he was the store manager, given the mustache, circa 1980.

"Yes, thanks. I'm about done, actually." Better to leave by choice than be thrown out for indecent exposure, right?

To her surprise, his face fell. "Oh. Well, uh, here's my card. If there's ever anything you want that we don't stock, just give me a call and I'll take care of you. I mean, I'll put in an order for you."

"Okay. Thanks." Her phone buzzed as she walked away.

Do you believe me yet? He grinned at her over a dessert display.

She shook her head and headed toward the front of the store.

I haven't checked out anyone else's junk, but I'm so hard from looking at you, I might have to violate this pie.

Her laugh was so loud, Mr. Mustache dropped his sticker gun. She tapped out: *Sorry your plan didn't have the effect you intended. It did have a side effect, though. Forget the pie and get me out of here.*

Braden must've sprinted across the parking lot, because he was waiting at the curb in his truck as soon as she had checked out. He hit the gas before she even had her seat belt on.

Lisa's jaw dropped when she saw the bulge in his jeans. "Wow. You weren't kidding." She ran a finger up and down his thigh. "Is all that for me?"

He took her hand and pressed it against his erection. "And lots more where that came from." She squeezed him and he made a sharp turn into an office complex. They thumped over a speed bump as he drove them past building after building.

"What are you doing?" The truck rocked to a stop in an empty dead-end parking area, in front of a building with a "for lease" sign.

He kissed her hard, almost viciously. "It's too long a drive. I won't make it." Unbuckling her seat belt, he dragged her across the seat to straddle him.

His mouth was delicious. She nipped at his lips and licked his tongue, rubbed her tits against his hard chest and rocked her aching cunt on his cock. He gathered the back of her shirt in a fist, pulling it tight against her breasts, further flaunting their hard, dusky tips to his hungry eyes. His hand slipped under her shirt to pluck at a nipple while he bit and sucked the other through the fabric.

Lisa pressed her crotch down on him, grinding, desperate for contact. "We've gotta be quick. If we get arrested, you might as well shoot me." Shifting to the side, she wiggled out of her shorts as he opened his jeans and freed his cock. She could smell her arousal and knew he could, too. Lowering herself to his lap, she slid her pussy along his hard shaft, audibly wet.

"Wait. Shit," he lifted her off of him. "I don't have a condom."

She groaned. "We could go back to the store... But you're clean, right?"

"Yeah. We got tested all the time for football. I haven't been celibate since then, but I've always used a condom."

"All right, well, I'm clean, too. Mostly from lack of use," she pouted. "And I can't get pregnant, so..."

"So." He lifted her by the hips and impaled her in one swift, smooth motion. They could hear how wet she was. "*Fuck* you feel good." He shoved her shirt up to toy with her breasts, flicking his tongue over one nipple then the other. With each flick, her pussy clenched, her clit throbbed.

Lisa planted her knees on either side of his hips, held onto his seat back, and raised and lowered herself, riding his cock. She gasped when the head of him rubbed her in just the right spot. "I'm gonna come on you," she panted. "I guess you don't need the heads-up so much since there's really no mess involved, but I thought you'd like to know."

She felt him smile as he nipped her neck. "Thanks for sharing. I'm close, too." Then he pistoned up into her, hard and deep. "In the interest of not getting caught, how 'bout we both... come... right... *now*."

Five minutes later, they were dressed and back on the road.

Braden grinned at her. "I can't believe that worked."

"When you get home, you're gonna register for the MCAT, right?"

"You call that pillow talk?" he grumbled.

"Do you see any pillows?"

He leered at her chest and she swatted his arm.

"No. I'm not."

She sputtered, "What? A deal's a deal! You made me do something really embarrassing, something I never would've done except-- Why are you laughing?" She swatted him again.

"I'm not gonna register when I get home, because I already did it."

Lisa brightened. "That's great! I'm so--" she gasped. "Oh my god! You're such a dick. Why did you make me do that?"

He gave her a sidelong glance and a slow, crooked smile.

She squirmed in her seat, ready for him again. "Dick," she grumbled.

* * *

"Are you gonna make me drag it out of you?" Natalie was giving her that look like she could see into her soul.

She had missed her friend and was happy to get the text that morning: *I can squeeze in a quick lunch if you're free.* Days ago, Lisa had been desperate to confide in her, but now... She froze with her sandwich halfway to her mouth.

"Drag what?"

"Your date with Thomas. Tell me." She popped a cherry tomato in her mouth. "But don't get graphic, 'cause I still have to work with him."

She relaxed a little. "It was nice. He's a nice guy."

Natalie stabbed at her salad. "That sounds boring as hell."

"We had a great dinner at that new fusion place. Riding in his convertible didn't turn my hair into a nest. That was a surprise. He walked me to the door, I kissed him on the cheek and that was it." She shrank as Nat studied her.

"You gonna see him again? 'Cause you look stressed. You need to get laid."

Lisa's belly laugh came out before she could stop it. She slapped a hand over her mouth.

Nat arched an eyebrow. "So you did sleep with him?"

"No. I did not sleep with Thomas." That last bite of turkey and swiss on rye felt like paste in her mouth.

Natalie narrowed her eyes, then lit up like a Christmas tree and leaned across the table. "Tell me *everything*. Don't skimp on the details."

"He's young and sweet and hot. We had sex," she shrugged, hoping it was enough.

"That bad, huh? A lot of fumbling around?"

She sighed. "He doesn't fumble."

Nat fixed her with a stare. "I work on the chain gang. I will never touch anything that beautiful. So for my own vicarious and prurient interest, you need to be a little more forthcoming with the info."

Lisa started at the beginning and caught her up on things, glossing over some of the more embarrassing aspects such as sprinklers, video chat and bralessness. "There. You happy? He's gorgeous, he's smart, and he knows his way around a vagina."

"Lucky," her friend pouted.

"It's terrifying, but I'm trying to think of it like a once-in-a-lifetime vacation to Hawaii or someplace." She played with the straw in her iced tea. "You can't stay forever and you can't come back, so you've gotta experience all of it while you're there. And even though you'll be heartbroken when it's time to check out and go home, the trip was totally worth it."

"So very, very lucky..." Nat sighed and checked her phone. "Crap. I have to get back."

They hugged on the sidewalk, agreeing to spend more time together once Natalie had her partnership in the bag.

<u>Chapter Twelve</u>

"'WHICH OF THE following is not a distinguishing characteristic of a species?'"

Lisa looked up from the MCAT review materials scattered across her kitchen table. Braden watched her with hungry eyes, idly rubbing his thumb through the condensation on his iced tea glass. She narrowed her eyes at him. "Are you with me here?"

"Yep. 'Which of the following is not a distinguishing characteristic of a species?'"

"Okay... Is it the sharing of a common gene pool; reproductive isolation from all other groups; ability to mate within the group--"

"Ability to mate within the group. Give me a harder one."

"They're all hard to me..." She skimmed the page. "'Which of the following vertebrate tissues or organs is best adapted for anaerobic respiration? Skeletal muscle; brain; cardiac muscle; or smooth muscle?'"

He thought a moment. "Skeletal?"

"Yeah, that's right. You're doing great so far."

Hooking a foot under her chair, he pulled her between his knees. "I've been studying. Like I promised." He scooped his hands under her ass and pulled her onto his lap, where her bottom was greeted by his growing erection. He pushed her chair away with his foot. "I think I deserve some positive reinforcement."

She squirmed against him while his mouth did delicious things to her neck. "Mm... you make a powerful argument," she conceded, sliding off his lap to kneel between his legs. She took her time unfastening his jeans, freeing his cock. "But you've been working so hard, it wouldn't be right for you to miss any study time..."

He pushed her hair off her face and melted her insides with a grin. "I'll be fine."

She continued as if he hadn't spoken, "I'm gonna take a little break, now, but while I'm on break, *you're* going to read the passage on cardiac imaging." She wrapped both hands around the thick base of him. "And when my break's over, I expect you to answer all the questions correctly."

"You're kidding."

She shrugged. "I guess I don't really need a break..."

His cock twitched in her hands. "Damn. You're kind of evil," he rasped and found the passage she'd assigned. "You gonna make me read out loud?"

"Up to you, long as you're able to take it all in." Her eyes sparkled as she placed a tiny kiss at the very tip of him. "My break starts when you start," she clarified, her lower lip brushing him as she spoke.

He glared down at her, then began reading, "'Cardiac radionuclide imaging is' -- *fuck* -- 'relatively easy to perform and exposes patients to--'" he growled as she took him to the back of her throat, "'--exposes patients to less radiation than comparable X-ray studies.'"

She hummed around him, enjoying his taste and his satiny hardness on her tongue.

"*Jesus*, you're good at that."

She lifted her mouth from him. Slick with saliva, his cock stood deeply flushed and granite-hard in her hands. "Keep reading," she smiled sweetly.

The struggle to focus on the words seemed to help him stave off his orgasm. He read the rest of the passage through gritted teeth, barely making it to the last paragraph. "'The volume of infracted, ischemic, and normal myocardium can be quantified, which is' -- *god*, if you don't move, I'm gonna come in your mouth."

Wordlessly communicating her intent, she deepened her suction and slipped a hand down to tug gently on his balls, one fingertip teasing the sensitive skin behind them.

The last words rushed out of him on a groan, "'--which is valuable in determining prognosis.' *Fuck!*" He tossed the book and grabbed her hair with both hands -- not that he needed to hold her in place. Her lips sealed around him as he pumped down her throat. She licked him clean and tucked him away as his grip on her hair gradually loosened.

Pushing off from his muscular thighs, she returned to her own chair. His long-lidded eyes widened a little when she wiped a drop from the corner of her mouth and sucked it from her fingertip.

Thinking back on it the next day, Lisa chuckled. The look on Braden's face when he had answered all the questions correctly was priceless. It came as no surprise to her -- she knew how smart he was. She was also not surprised when he laid her out on the kitchen table and tried to convince her to help him study like that all through med school, if he got in. He was damned persuasive, but Lisa was pretty sure she'd not made any promises she couldn't keep.

At least, she hadn't before he made stars explode in her head. And after that, she wasn't really capable of speech. Hell, she was still on the table and had barely opened her eyes when he'd kissed her goodbye and left for work.

His bar tending job was a godsend, she thought. She loved spending time with him -- both naked and not -- and more than she should. It was just as well he worked most nights, since, in the name of self-preservation, she couldn't let him spend the night in her bed. In three years, no one but she and Jake had slept in her home.

Jake. She logged into her bank account and cringed. Having her fees cut had made the bleak financial landscape bleaker. She paid a couple of late bills, then sent as much to Jake's camp as she could without bouncing the mortgage payment. It wasn't the full amount owed, but hopefully the camp director would appreciate her effort and not send Jake home early. Although Vance was apparently ignoring personal email while in Europe, she sent him another scathing note, anyway. She prayed Jake's summer wouldn't be ruined by his dad's selfishness.

The next weeks were busy with underpaid and over-dull catalogue work. She didn't see Braden much, as his test date was approaching and he needed to study for the physical sciences section. The complex formulas and chemistry made her head spin, but he seemed to have a good grasp of it.

Lisa had wished him luck the night before the MCAT, not that he needed it. Braden was so sharply intelligent, it was sad how few people acknowledged the brilliant mind tucked inside that gorgeous man. He called on his way home from the test, exhausted but confident he had done well. She was proud that he was finally willing to embrace his own intellect. One day soon, when he went off to med school and Lisa was left wrecked and alone, she would find comfort in knowing she did that for him.

She had expected him to sleep for a week after the exam, but sometime the next morning he showed up to trim her hedges. He must not have wanted to wake her, because she didn't even know he was out there until she was sipping her first cup of coffee. She watched him through the kitchen window as she had a month ago, admiring the glistening muscles of his sweat-slicked chest and arms.

And as she did a month ago, she brought him a glass of tea. "Good morning, Doctor."

"Thanks, beautiful. I didn't wake you, did I?" As always, his dimpled grin dampened her panties.

"Nope. But I wouldn't have minded if you did." She watched him drain the tall glass in four deep swallows. Condensation dripped on his chest, but unlike when that happened a month ago, she didn't pretend not to notice. Instead, she followed its trail with her tongue, and felt his whole body harden as he hissed in a breath. Taking the cold, empty glass, she drew a wet line on him connecting one tight nipple to the other, then down the ridges of his hard stomach to trace the low waistband of his shorts.

"No, ma'am." He captured her hand before it could palm his erection. "I've missed you too much to fuck you on a lawn chair." His thumb stroked her palm, sending a tingle directly her clit. "Let me go home and grab a quick shower. And when I get back, I'm gonna take my time with you." His eyes and voice were so full of intent, she felt herself cream.

"That sounds promising, except the part where you leave. I'll throw your clothes in the wash and you can shower here." She took her hand from his grasp and stroked his hard-on where it tented his shorts. "I'd buy a ticket to see that."

Her master bathroom wasn't huge, but she had always loved the shower. With its thick, clear glass walls, built-in bench and rainfall shower head, it had the feel of a private spa. It was where she was best able to relax -- in part, because the separate hand-held sprayer had practically been her boyfriend the last three years.

When Lisa came back from tossing in the laundry, the bathroom door was wide open and the shower was going. The steamy air smelled like sunflowers. Braden's eyes were closed, his head tipped back as he rinsed shampoo from his hair. She sat on the counter and watched the sudsy water sluice over every perfect golden inch of him. His penis stood at half-mast, and she wondered if he was *ever* fully-flaccid.

She must've made a noise because his eyes popped open, wet lashes dark and spiky over the deep blue-green. His bee-stung lips curved in sexy invitation. "You look dirty. I think you'd best get in here." He worked the bar of soap into a lather. Much like he did to her.

"Nope, I'm clean. Only my mind is dirty." No way was she going to strip for him in the brightly-lit bathroom. It was embarrassing enough letting him see her by the light of the little bedside lamp.

He gripped his hardening cock, soaping it with slow, sudsy strokes. "I'll make it worth your while."

Lisa's mouth went dry and she clenched her jaw. Her hands itched to lather him up. Her breasts swelled at the thought of him doing the same to her. "No, thanks. I'm enjoying the show from here."

His eyes narrowed at her, but he dropped the subject -- as well as the object of their mutual affection. He looked disappointed. Hell, she was disappointed, too. He rinsed off quickly and efficiently. *Show's over*, she sighed. When he opened the shower door, she handed him a towel, not daring to make eye contact.

"I'm sorry," she murmured. "Are you mad?"

"Yeah. I am." He wrapped the towel around his waist, then took her neck between his warm, damp hands and stroked her jaw with his thumbs. His eyes were a riot of emotion. "But not at you. I'm pissed at Vance. At Hollywood. At fashion magazines. Whoever's responsible for you not knowing how absolutely fucking beautiful you are." Thank god he kissed her then, else he might've seen the tears before she could blink them back.

Hours later, Braden had more than made good on his promise to take his time with her. They had started in the bedroom, then he'd followed her into the laundry room and they spent some time there working up a thirst, so they made a detour to the kitchen, and ultimately settled on the soft living room rug with Lisa's head resting on his chest.

He idly ran his fingers through her hair. "Thank you."

"I think I should be thanking *you.*"

"Not for that," he chuckled. "I want you to know I really appreciate how you push me, believe in me." She kissed his chest, too sated to move. He continued, "You got me to re-take the MCAT, something I never thought I'd do. And you know, the studying was hard, but I didn't really mind it. I feel different. Smarter."

"I'm glad," she smiled, drowsily.

"It's all thanks to you. And now I'm ready to negotiate for my med school applications."

"We settled all that at Kroger, remember?"

"I remember explaining that applications would be a separate negotiation."

She scowled. "That's unfair, considering how you duped me last time."

"I won't dupe you again."

"Do I get to wear a bra this time?" she teased.

"No. You get to wear nothing."

"I'm wearing nothing, now, so I guess I've upheld my side of the bargain."

He pinched her ass. "If you want me to apply to med schools, you'll model nude for a life drawing class." She couldn't see his face, but his voice was serious.

She sat up and hugged a throw pillow as a shield. "You think embarrassing the hell out of me will improve my self-image?" In theory, it sounded kind of sexy. The idea of actually doing it, however, sounded like something out of a nightmare.

"I took life drawing as an elective last year. No one cares what you look like, whether it's my image of you or yours. Their models are all ages, shapes and sizes. The artists are respectful. It's not a sexual atmosphere at all."

She was confused. "So why do you want me to do it?"

He started to pry the throw pillow away from her, then sighed and let her hang onto it. After what seemed like a struggle to choose his words, he said, "Because I love your body, and I want you to love it, too."

Chapter Thirteen

"WHEN YOU STAND on platform, I pose you. I will not touch your *parties intimes,* your lady parts." The diminutive professor had hair like Albert Einstein and a voice like Pepe LePew. He snickered and continued, "I put you in *la posture, et* you be very still, *oui?*"

"Yes," Lisa agreed. The sweet older man put her at ease, but she was still nervous. *Well, who wouldn't be?* she thought. She was naked under her bathrobe, minutes from dropping said robe in front of the thirty or so university art students who were filing in. For a moment, she regretted asking Braden not to come.

How did he talk her into this? She didn't truly believe he would refuse to apply to med school if she hadn't agreed. So why was she here? Because even with the humiliation, somewhere in the back of her demented little mind the idea turned her on. She was hyper-aware of the terrycloth robe rubbing her hard nipples, and hoped to hell she wouldn't be positioned in a way that the students could see how wet and swollen she was.

In the center of the room, the platform was draped in a white sheet with a couple of white pillows on top. When the professor led her there, the students hardly glanced up. They were all readying their easels and drawing supplies.

"We start with one minute and work up to longer session." He stacked the pillows. "Sit here, lean back on pillows, knees bent to that side."

"Okay," she nodded. Her heart was thumping and her ponytail felt too tight.

"*Tres bien.*" He addressed the class and gave them their assignment, then gestured to Lisa. She took a deep breath and dropped her robe.

She lowered herself to the pedestal as gracefully as possible, considering that thirty strangers could see every naked inch of her excessively-curvy forty-one year-old body. A twinge of embarrassment touched her, but it felt artificial and muted, like it was brought on only because she had *expected* to feel embarrassment. Like when a sneeze sneaks away, but you make the noise anyhow.

The professor put on some soft music while Lisa reclined on the pillows. He adjusted the position of her legs, straightening one more than the other and tipped her chin down and to the left. Once satisfied with her pose, he confirmed that she was comfortable, then he set his timer for one minute.

Her heart rate slowed to normal surprisingly quickly. It helped that the artists were focused on their work. Most simply glanced her way occasionally for reference. No one stared or ogled, so she didn't feel judged.

For the second pose, the professor asked her to stand with her hands on her ponytail, as if she were pulling it through the elastic. "Is only one minute, so your arms no fall off," he chuckled. Holding her arms up like that forced her back to arch and pushed her breasts up. For sixty seconds, she stood still as a statue -- a naked statue with an audience of strangers.

When she and Braden had discussed this scenario, she was privately worried her arousal would drip noticeably down her thighs. In reality, the atmosphere was so completely nonsexual that despite her nudity her body was oddly relaxed. In fact, she found the whole experience rather meditative.

The longer poses were more challenging. One semi-reclining pose had her lying on her belly, propped on her elbows with her chest off the floor as if she were reading at the beach. By the time twenty minutes was up, she had developed an ache in one shoulder and her hand was going numb. Luckily, the professor gave the class a break, so she was able to get her blood circulating again.

She pulled on her robe and sipped a bottle of water. Most of the students had left the room, but a pretty artist with long blonde dreadlocks got her attention with a friendly smile. "Thanks for sitting for us. Is this your first time?"

Lisa laughed. "That obvious?"

"Not at all, I've just never drawn you before," the artist chuckled. "You're a great subject. Would you like to see?"

She had survived posing naked for strangers, but seeing those strangers' impressions of her naked body was only asking to have her self-esteem punched in the neck. "No, that's okay," she hedged.

The younger woman gave her a knowing look. "You've got nothing to be afraid of."

She hesitated a moment, then walked around the easel. There were a number of bare-bones drawings on the sketchpad, various poses of a graceful woman with lush breasts, nicely-rounded hips and a tiny waist. Lisa found it hard to believe the subject of the drawings was supposed to be her. Maybe the nice hippie chick was high.

Lisa smiled politely and looked at the next easel. And the next. And despite variations in style and perspective, every drawing depicted the same graceful woman with lush breasts, nicely-rounded hips and a tiny waist. After circling the room, seeing her naked self through so many artists' eyes, she had to blink back tears.

For the first time in her life, she felt beautiful.

The university was close to an hour away, so by the time she got home it was early evening. When she took her phone from her bag, she saw she had gotten a text from Braden: *Well? Should I start filling out applications?*

Yes, but you can start tomorrow. Come over?

On my way.

She poured a glass of Chardonnay and drank it all in the five minutes it took him to get there. His sandy hair was windblown, and his snug t-shirt emphasized his sculpted chest and lean waist. Well-worn jeans hugged his thighs and the conspicuous bulge of his crotch. The sexy, woodsy male scent of him made her mouth water.

As soon as he had closed the door behind him, she pressed him back against it with her hands on his hard stomach.

"I take it you're not mad at me for making you do that," he rumbled down at her, flashing a lust-inducing dimple.

"Not mad. Thank you," she said, licking and nibbling his lips.

"Mm... you're welcome, beautiful." He slanted his mouth over hers. When he deepened the kiss, she pulled away, tugging his hand so he would follow her down the hall.

In the bedroom, she tossed her blouse on a chair and shimmied out of her jeans. He leaned in the doorway, watching with hot eyes as she unfastened the front hook of her bra and let her breasts spill out. She turned away from him and bent, slowly dragging her panties down her legs. From the low groan behind her, she knew he was looking at her puffy, wet folds. Steam billowed from the bathroom when she pushed open the door. "I'm ready for that shower, now," she said huskily.

He came in and closed the door as she stepped under the water. She squirted jasmine-scented body wash in her hands, and soaped her breasts and belly without ever looking away from him. The hunger on his face fed her soul. His eyes devoured her and he didn't blink once as he pulled his shirt over his head and kicked off his jeans. Cold air further tightened her already-hard nipples when he opened the glass enclosure and joined her under the spray.

His wet mouth was possibly the most delicious thing she'd ever tasted. His wet body was definitely the most perfect thing she'd ever touched.

He took her soapy breasts in his big hands, lifting and pressing them together, tugging her slick nipples between his fingers. She drizzled body wash down her chest and he made good use of it, thoroughly covering her in slippery bubbles.

"God, you've got gorgeous tits," he murmured. She felt her clit swell as if he were working it with a phantom third hand.

His erection nudged her belly. She poured body wash into her palm and smoothed it up and down his rigid cock, watching the lather build as he grew even harder with each sudsy stroke. When she switched on the hand-held shower head, he gave her a quizzical look.

The twinkle in her big brown eyes accompanied an impish smile. "I want to suck you, but I don't think that warrants having my mouth washed out with soap." She went to her knees and ran the spray over the thick length in her hand, rinsing him clean.

He rubbed a wet thumb across her lips and pushed it between them, grunting a little when she sucked on it before he withdrew. "Yeah, I like your dirty mouth just the way it is."

She brought his penis to her lips and swirled her tongue around the crown, licking the water off. Before she could take him deeper, he peeled her tight fingers from him and took his cock in hand, tracing her lips with the plump, rosy head.

"Just your mouth."

Her tongue darted out and caught a taste of him before he moved out of reach. "You overestimate me if you think I can keep my hands off you."

"Well find something else to do with them, 'cause I'm gonna feed you my cock."

The words made her pussy clench and she purred like a tiger cub. She clasped her hands at her back and dutifully opened her mouth to receive him. Even with the shower raining down on her ass, she could feel her slick arousal on her inner thighs.

True to his word, he held his cock to her parted lips and pressed inside. "Look at you... Jesus, you're so fucking hot." He fed himself to her slowly, two inches forward, one inch back, until he bumped the back of her throat. She arched her back and rubbed her breasts against him, enjoying the way the light brown hair on his thighs abraded her nipples.

Raising her eyes, she found him watching intently. Rivulets ran over his chest and stomach, down his wrist to the hand that held his cock at Lisa's mouth, where she sipped and sucked the water from him. She covered her teeth with her lips and gave him a long, tight stroke.

He slid his thumb lower, and she swirled her tongue over it, then sucked it in with the rest of him. His nostrils flared and his eyes went full black. The thick shaft in her mouth was so hard, it almost didn't feel human. With his free hand, he grabbed her wet hair.

"Stop. I don't want to come before you do."

She sucked harder, looking up at him with black-brown eyes and hollowed cheeks. When he would've pulled away, she grabbed his ass with both hands and held him there.

"*God Lisa*," he rasped. "Careful, I'm-- *fuck!*"

The moment she felt him tighten she released his cock from her mouth, covered his hand with both of hers, and jacked him off until he covered her breasts in hot, white bursts.

Panting, he sank down to the built-in bench and gave her a heated glare. "You're gonna pay for that. When I can move again. In a few minutes."

"Promises, promises," she muttered, drawing a menacing look from him. She stood under the rain shower until all visible traces of him were gone from her skin.

"You call that clean?" he taunted.

She grinned and soaped herself up for him again. "This thorough enough for you?" Her eyes widened when his dick began to twitch awake. *Mmm... the joys of youth.*

"Guess it'll do," he said with a slow smile. He stood and turned on the hand-held sprayer. "You washed, I'll rinse. Sit."

Lisa knew sitting was maybe not the most flattering position, but she wasn't given much choice when he put a hand on her chest and gently pushed her down on the bench. She sat up straight with her hands on her knees as he ran the sprayer across her soapy breasts, watching millions of iridescent bubbles slide down her belly into her lap.

He held the sprayer away and looked pointedly at the tight seam between her thighs. "Open for me."

She let her legs relax a little.

"Wider."

She opened wider.

"More."

She gave him a little more.

Big hands gripped her knees and shoved them apart. "There. Stay." He licked his lips as his gaze slid over her exposed pussy.

Lisa thought she could probably come with nothing but his eyes on her.

But she forgot that thought and all others when he flicked the spray over her swollen cunt. Her knees closed of their own volition and he pushed them open again.

"I said *stay*," he reminded her.

"I'll try," she promised.

"Not good enough." He glanced around, then removed the cap from the body wash and balanced it on her left knee. He unscrewed the shampoo cap and set it on her right knee. "Drop them if you want me to stop." His grin was evil and sexy as all hell as he brought the spray back around.

"Oh god," she whispered.

Braden made the water lick her from thigh to thigh, teasing her clit. Her knees shook and the shampoo cap fell. He chuckled as she caught and replaced it before it hit the tile. His eyes followed the spray as he drew it over her in a lazy figure eight.

"I love how your pretty little clit gets so hard for me."

The clit in question was pounding. Lisa bit her lip, struggling to keep her legs from shaking.

"I bet you get yourself off like this," he ran the spray across her breasts then back over her cunt. "Am I right?"

"Yes," she gasped and rubbed her nipples. The water needles had made them ache.

"I'd like to see that." He dropped the sprayer and went to his knees. "Some other time, though," he murmured before he sank his tongue into her.

Two caps hit the floor, but nobody noticed or cared.

He pulled her knees over his shoulders and lifted her off the bench, licking her from back to front. When he set her back down, he fingered the neat little patch of dark blonde hair she had left on top of her shaved pussy. "I like this."

She didn't think any more blood could rush to that part of her body until he wrapped his soft lips around her clit and tugged it into his hot mouth, sucking in time to her pounding heart before releasing her. "I *love* this." Very lightly, he nibbled and kissed and nuzzled her until she heard herself making incoherent sounds of need.

With a growl, he pulled her clit back into his mouth, sucking with hard pulses, grabbing her ass with both hands to hold her in place when she bucked away. Her orgasm overtook her and she came in great, wet waves, which he lapped up with a greedy tongue.

Chapter Fourteen

LISA HELD THE phone at arm's length so as not to be deafened by Natalie's joyful screech. If her friend was this happy to hear that Lisa had dropped her catalogue client, she could only imagine the screaming if she were to tell her about The Shower. Luckily, she had no plans to do so.

"It's about damn time! If they cut your rates any more, you'd be paying *them* to shoot their frigging staplers."

"Just about," she said distractedly. Her studio felt too big and empty without all the stacks of office equipment and supplies.

"I'm so happy for you. Who will you be shooting for now?"

"Um, me."

"Well yeah, I know how freelance works, but who hired you?"

The butterflies in Lisa's stomach started acting up again, flying around and fretting about money. She ignored the flitty little bastards and idly straightened a reflective umbrella, forcing a confident smile. "Nobody. I'm worth more than what catalogue gigs will pay, so from now on I'm shooting for myself."

"That's awesome, Lise." Nat's honest excitement for Lisa came through loud and clear, tinged with subtle tones of awe and envy. "Now you'll have plenty of time to shoot sexy vegetables and build your photo stock."

She snorted. "Too bad there's not a lot of call for that kind of thing."

"Didn't Thomas order a few prints?"

"Yeah, that covered last month's electric bill. Now I only need four or five hundred more print orders and I might make a living." Last week, Thomas had asked Lisa to come by the office to collect her portfolio and his print order. While she was there he had invited her to lunch, and she made a weak excuse about rushing to meet a client-imposed deadline. He was nice, handsome, successful, and close to her own age. He was everything she should want, but she couldn't have been less interested. "Hey, uh... maybe don't mention to Thomas that I quit the catalogue gig," she added.

Nat made a frowny noise. "How long do you plan to use that excuse? Just tell him you're not into him. In a nice way."

"But I want to be into him. I should be into him!" She stomped her foot in frustration. "Why am I not into him?"

The woman purported to be her best friend in the world laughed at her. *Laughed* at her! "You know damn well why, and you won't be getting any sympathy from me. At least, not until I see some photo evidence."

When they hung up so Nat could get back to work, Lisa tried to relax and soak up the vibe of the studio. Three years ago, she had fallen in love with the funky old building which had housed creatives for decades. The rent was too high on the standard two-year lease, but she had so needed the history and energy of the place that she signed an extended five-year lease for a reduced monthly payment.

With a scowl, she remembered the condescending lecture Vance gave her that night about over-committing. She refused to consider that he might have been right. Sure, she had two more years on the lease and no income to speak of, but she had talent and a unique point of view. She would find a way to channel that into a career. Hopefully before being evicted.

She took a deep breath. *Freedom!* She finally had the freedom to take the kind of pictures she'd always wanted to take, to shoot the things she had always wanted to shoot. The possibilities were infinite! She had so many choices.

Too many. It was overwhelming, actually, the more she thought about it.

And kind of depressing, for some reason.

And terrifying.

Really terrifying.

By the time she got home, the cry of the money-anxious butterflies in her stomach had reached a crescendo. A glass of wine did nothing to calm her nerves, but she knew a second glass on an empty stomach would do more harm than good. *What kind of moron drops a bread-and-butter client without a back-up?* She was in no position to be choosy. Where did she get such an over-inflated opinion of herself?

Braden. She wanted to blame him, but it wasn't his fault she had gotten too caught up in the fantasy they were spinning. She was the idiot who'd bought into his vision of her. And now, what began as a sexy diversion was messing with her head in a dangerous way.

Vance and Elena would be home in a couple weeks. Jake, a week after that if she could hold off the camp enforcer a bit longer. They had never discussed it, but obviously she and Braden couldn't continue seeing each other once everyone was back in town. Her throat tightened at the thought. If she ended it now, at least she would have some time to get over him a little before she had to put on a happy face for Jake.

With impeccable timing, her phone buzzed: *How was your day, beautiful?*

Tears pricked her eyes. She already missed the way he made her feel.

Lisa? You there?

If she responded, she'd have to tell him and it would be over. Her heart hurt as she turned off the phone and left it in the kitchen where it all began.

Half an hour later, after a quick cry and a minor panic attack, she was in her office desperately trying to goose the muse with loud music and internet loitering. There was no getting her client back, so she had to move forward. She had no other choice. But how could she establish herself as a professional photographer when she wasn't motivated to take any pictures? Nothing got her excited enough to pick up a camera. Her jaw ached from frustrated clenching. She closed her eyes and tried to massage the muscles the way Braden had taught her.

"Knock-knock."

She jumped with a shriek. "Shit, you scared me to death!"

"Sorry to barge in." Gorgeously disheveled, Braden stood in the doorway. Lisa's heart thumped as she turned off the music, glad to have the desk between them. He set her phone on the desk. "Everything all right? You didn't respond to my texts, and my calls went straight to voicemail."

Her eyes flicked to the phone, still powered off as she'd left it. "It died when I got home. Guess I forgot to plug it in." She connected the charger and powered on the phone, angling it so he wouldn't see that it was almost fully charged. *Five missed calls. Three voicemail messages.* "Sorry to worry you. Everything's fine, as you can see."

He didn't seem to buy that as he sank into her old red sofa. "Listen to the messages. Put it on speaker."

"Okay..." She was apprehensive, but set the phone on the desk and played her messages.

Braden's voice said, *"Hey beautiful, it's me. Everything okay? It says you read my texts, but you didn't respond, so... I'll try back in a few."*

She tried to cover. "Right. Yeah, I was about to text you back when it died. My brain's scrambled. It was kind of a rough day." At least the last part was true.

Before he could answer, the next message began. *"Mrs. Taylor, this is Paul at Camp Big League. Again. We need to make arrangements for you to pick Jake up this week, unless you plan to remit payment--"* She grabbed the phone and stopped the message.

Braden frowned. "I thought he's at camp 'til the end of the month."

Lisa debated how much to blast Vance to his stepson. "He is. Someone got their wires crossed. I'm working it out," she hedged.

"What's to work out? Vance pays for camp, right?"

"That was the agreement," she sighed. "I've emailed and left messages, but I guess he's not checking all that on vacation."

"My mom's been in touch. I'll tell her--"

"And how would you explain this conversation? As far as they know, I haven't seen you in years."

"I'll say you left a message at the house. She'll make him take care of it."

That was logical. She relaxed a little. "Okay... yeah. Thank you. Jake would be devastated if he had to come home early."

He leaned forward and looked at her intently. "Well, I'm not quite ready for him to come home yet, either."

Shit. Shit-shit-shit. He gave her the opening, so she had to use it. "Braden... I think we need to stop seeing each other."

"Like hell we do." He stood and planted his palms on her desk, looming over her. "What's going on?"

"I just don't have room in my life for... *this*... right now." Before he interrupted, she continued, "Apparently, I went temporarily insane and dropped my catalogue client to do my own thing. So as of this afternoon, I've got no income until I take a bunch of new pictures and sell them."

"But that's great." He looked truly happy for her.

"No, it isn't." She made a frustrated noise. "It was a huge mistake. I've got no inspiration. I can't think of anything I want to shoot."

Braden looked at the framed prints hanging around her office. "Well... where'd you get the idea for the squash?"

"I looked in my shopping cart."

He grinned at her flat tone. "All right. How about the park bench?"

"Walked by it. Thought it was cool." She sighed. "If I'm gonna build a business I need to do a series... something I can put my stamp on. It was stupid to drop my only source of income before I had a plan." She watched him study each of her prints, could see his wheels turning.

"Well, the thing I love most in your work is how you make me see stuff in a unique way... like the shadows on the bench, the curves of the squash..."

It was so nice to be appreciated for the thing she liked best about herself, Lisa felt almost safe for a moment. "Yeah, I've been brainstorming stuff that would look cool in a really tight shot. So far, nothing comes to mind that would lend itself to a cohesive series."

"Maybe you're coming at it from the wrong direction. Instead of looking at the whole, then reducing it to a small part of that... what if you start with the part and only hint at the whole?"

"Hm..." she said thoughtfully. "Keep talking."

"Okay... you want images that grab someone's attention... Like, you could take the world's coolest picture of a hub cap, but so what?"

"Exactly," she nodded.

"Small part of a larger whole..." he mused. "And I think it should be the kind of thing that forces an emotional response, y'know what I mean?"

She sat forward in her chair, loving the energy that came with spitballing on the right track. "Yeah, it's gotta be... provocative... like a sharp blade..."

"Or a nipple."

"Seriously," she chuckled, though he didn't seem to be kidding.

"Seriously. The image of your nipple stuck with me for ten years, and not just because I was a horny kid. It's a small part that hints at the whole... it's provocative, and there are plenty more body parts to build a series on."

She felt herself blush. "I am not taking pictures of my nipple."

He shrugged. "So take pictures of mine."

Lisa stared at him. It was a good idea. And he did have plenty of provocative parts.

Chapter Fifteen

THE PLAY OF light and shadow over sculpted muscle was deliciously intriguing. Lisa adjusted the umbrella to reduce the fill light, carving deeper shadows into the oblique muscles along Braden's ribcage.

"Sorry I don't have anything more comfortable for you to sit on. My last models were printers and fax machines."

Braden gave her a provocative smile from atop the white fabric-draped work table. "I'm good. Just get what you need." He thumbed the waistband of his underwear and looked up at her from under his lashes. "Sure you don't want these off?"

Per her earlier request, the boxer-briefs now sat halfway down his hips, low enough to reveal where his deep V-cut abs disappeared into shadowy pubic hair. She eyed his partial erection with a rueful smile. "No, but I'm sure I won't get many more pictures taken if you aren't wearing them."

His answering grin confirmed her decision.

As it was, she did ultimately ask him to lose the boxers. His ass was simply too perfect to exclude from the series. She shot a few angles of his gorgeous backside before he shifted.

"Don't move yet -- let me get a couple more."

"Sorry." Braden rolled to face her, carefully freeing a full erection from under his hip. "I can't lie on my stomach right now, unless you wanna cut a glory hole in your table."

She blinked. "Oddly enough, this was never an issue for the printers and fax machines."

His dick looked painfully hard. It jerked and he gripped the base in a tight fist. To keep it in check, she supposed. Whatever the reason, seeing his strong hand wrapped around it made her mouth go dry and her panties damp.

And he knew it, the brat. Lisa could see in his eyes that he knew what he was doing to her, even before his hand made a slow journey over the length of his shaft to tug the swollen head of him. There was an answering tug in her core, and she gasped a little.

The glint in his eye went from mischievous to predatory in an instant. "If you need any more before I haul you onto this table, you'd better get them quick," he said in a deep rasp.

"I know. Jesus, I know." She wiped a damp palm on her jeans and pivoted the tripod head to a new angle. "I only want one. Squeeze it for me," she whispered.

His brow furrowed as he did, and the muscles of his forearm and bicep bunched the way they'd done when she watched him on the lounge chair and in video chat.

Composition was everything. Of course she could crop it later if necessary, but for the shot she wanted it would feel like cheating. She checked the viewfinder and captured him from wrist to shoulder, hoping for an innocuous picture that suggestively implied what was happening just out of frame. Working quickly, she was able to snap a few before he grabbed her arm and yanked her on top of him.

* * *

Lisa popped the memory card into her computer and waited impatiently for the pictures to load. As soon as they'd returned from the studio Braden left for work and she had rushed into her office, too anxious to waste time rinsing off their sex or even grabbing a drink. One by one, the thumbnails came up, until her monitor was one big contact sheet. She made herself view them in order, despite how much she was dying to start at the end.

Having never done a shoot like this before she was afraid to expect much, but she needn't have worried. The pictures were beautiful. Smooth, golden skin wrapped around the gorgeous body that only an hour ago was wrapped around her. Halfway through the set, she already knew this was the best work she had ever done.

Clicking through the pictures, she slowed as she neared the end. There were at least a dozen she planned to use, but she had high hopes for the last set-up. She braced herself and opened one. "Oh my god..." Even without correction or cropping, it was fantastic. The muscles of Braden's arm bunched just enough to force the viewer to imagine what was left unseen.

The artist in her would spend the rest of the night tweaking mid-tones, color and framing so she'd be ready to upload the new stock photos tomorrow. But first, her giddy inner girl sent a quick email to Natalie, eager to share her excitement and favorite shots with her best friend. Not surprisingly, Natalie called -- screaming her own excitement -- a few minutes later.

Once Lisa posted the new gallery, it quickly became apparent that descriptors like "sexy man" and "partial nude" were lots more popular than "park bench" or "squash." Seemed a no-brainer in retrospect, but she wasn't complaining. In the first week, she sold more prints and digital use rights of the Braden images than she had of all her other stock photo sales combined.

She insisted Braden accept a model's fee, since the pictures were selling so well. He was on her red sofa with his laptop, working on med school applications when she brought it up. It was almost an argument, until she showed him her sales log to prove how much she was earning.

"If it keeps up, maybe you can quit tending bar."

"That'd be great, but not while I'm crashing at my mom's. She'd wonder where I was getting the money."

"Crap. You're right." They had agreed never to tell their families that he'd modeled for her, and none of the pictures showed his face to ensure his identity stayed hidden.

They worked on their respective computers in comfortable silence for a while, then an email notification popped up on Lisa's screen. She didn't recognize the sender's name and almost deleted it unread, until she realized it was sent from one of the biggest ad agencies in the country. The subject line read "Your Photos." She skimmed the message and gasped.

Braden looked at her over his laptop. "You okay?"

"Listen to this," she grinned. "'Dear Ms. Taylor, I am heading up a new marketing campaign for Allister & Hitch Apparel. In our search for the new face of our brand, we came across your excellent photos of a faceless -- but otherwise ideal -- male model.'"

"Holy shit."

"I know! Then he says 'I'd be much obliged if you would forward his head shot and contact information. With warm regards, Declan Reece, Creative Director.'"

"Wild. Think it's legit?"

She shrugged. "Seems to be. Want me to respond?"

"Sure. I don't have a head shot, though."

"That's all right. I think I've got one or two that could work..." Lisa turned back to her monitor to hide the flush in her cheeks. Despite knowing she wouldn't use them in her stock gallery, she had taken quite a few shots of his beautiful face. She knew she'd want them when he was gone.

After previewing a few, she found her favorite. It was framed from head to hips. He had been on his back and was in the process of sitting up, so his arms were flexed, abs tight. His deep blue-green eyes stared out of the picture and straight into her soul. That sinful mouth looked kissably soft, lips parted just a little, giving him a slight vulnerability. She turned the monitor.

"This one okay with you?"

"I don't fucking know," he laughed, embarrassed. "Do you like it?"

"Yes. I like it."

"Great. Let's roll the dice."

She added a watermark to the photo to protect her copyright, then sent it with a reply including Braden's name and phone number. "Okay. The dice have been rolled. Now get back to those applications, Kate Moss."

Braden's chuckle was low and suggestive. "I like it when you're strict, Ms. Taylor." He dragged his hot gaze to her mouth, down her neck and over her breasts. She felt it physically, nipples peaking like they'd been teased by his fingertips.

He set his laptop aside and stood behind her desk chair. Gently sweeping her hair to one side, he fastened his mouth on her neck, working his way down to her shoulder with warm, wet suction. She gave a little moan when his hands slid down from her shoulders to cover her breasts. He cupped her lightly, letting her nipples scrape his palms.

Right when the throbbing began between her legs, he removed his hands and spun her chair to face him. She grabbed his face and devoured his mouth, loving the slide of his tongue, the nip of his teeth, the growl in his throat. He ended the kiss by shoving her chair back.

Dropping to his knees, he pushed her shirt up and pulled a taut nipple into his mouth through her pale blue bra. His big hands held hers on the arms of the chair, trapping her in place as he worked one nipple then the other with his teeth and tongue. She squirmed in her seat, tight nipples straining against wet blue satin. He pulled the chair closer and bent to position his mouth on the seam of her jeans, directly over her clit. Through the heavy denim, she felt him nip at her and she rocked her hips toward him. It took a few seconds to realize the pulsing rhythm in her head was his phone ringing. She pushed at his shoulders.

"Your phone. Braden, your phone."

"So?"

"It might be your mom. They're on their way home, right?"

He sat back on his heels and stood, pulling the phone from his pocket in the same motion. With a glance at the screen, he shrugged and answered, "Hello, this is Braden."

Lisa tugged her shirt down. She heard a man's deep voice coming through the phone, but couldn't tell what was being said.

Braden pointed to the computer, mouthing, *It's him.*

She smiled then listened impatiently to one side of the conversation.

"Hi, yeah. She said you might call... Okay... Uh-huh... Not far at all, we're in Dunwoody..." He chuckled and began to pace with the phone. "No. I was a football player. I recently graduated from UGA and I'm applying to med schools now..." He winked at Lisa and she heard the deep pitch of Declan's voice expressing surprise. He listened a while longer, then his eyebrows raised, "That sounds great, as long as Lisa's the photographer."

She waved her arms to get Braden's attention and hissed, "*No!*"

He ignored her and continued on the phone, "What you saw was all the modeling I've ever done. I wouldn't really be comfortable working with anyone else... I understand..."

Lisa covered her face with her hands. Braden had just blown a tremendous opportunity out of loyalty to her. She didn't know whether to kill him or kiss him.

"Sure, of course. I get it... You too, thanks."

After he disconnected the call, she shook her head and sighed. "I know you were trying to help me, but I wish you hadn't. A modeling gig like that would've covered a lot of med school tuition."

"Yeah, you're probably right."

"I *am* right," she scowled. "So why are you grinning like a doofus?"

His eyes twinkled. "'Cause he wants to meet us in a few days to go over contracts and take some test shots."

<u>Chapter Sixteen</u>

LESS THAN A week later, test shots had been approved and contracts had been signed.

Braden was still in the stylist's chair when Lisa arrived at the agency's downtown Atlanta studio. They'd driven separately, since he had to be there two hours earlier for hair and wardrobe. Plus, they'd agreed not to tell their new employer about their personal relationship, and showing up together would arouse suspicion. Not to mention, Vance and Elena were home, so carpooling was out of the question.

The stylist, a gorgeous girl with ebony skin and natural hair, unclasped a smock from Braden's shoulders. "Remember baby, don't touch your hair or I'll have to break your fingers."

"I got it," he laughed, then his eyes met Lisa's in the mirror. "Hey, Lisa, this is Kimani. I thought she was cool until she put makeup on me."

Kimani flashed a bright smile at Lisa. "You know this clown?"

"Since he was about half that size," Lisa chuckled.

When Kimani left them alone to make a coffee run, Lisa and Braden stood awkwardly, maintaining an impersonal distance in case anyone walked in.

"This is crazy, huh?" He shook his head in amazement.

"Uh, yeah. You were already gorgeous, but Christ..." she murmured, staring.

He was bare-chested under an open, long-sleeved shirt, and wore a pair of crotch-hugging jeans she recognized as Allister & Hitch brand. His hair had been carefully styled to look windblown. Or bed-tumbled.

His grin heated the chilly studio. "We've got some time to kill..."

"And risk ruining your makeup? No way," she teased. "Anyhow, I saw Ivy on my way in. She said Declan should be down in a few." Lisa liked Ivy, Declan's goth-looking, über-efficient assistant. She had done a great job handling the contracts and test-shots when Declan was called out of town at the last minute. Still, after communicating practically non-stop with him since that first email, it would be nice to finally meet the guy in person.

"You're gonna pay for that remark." Braden's eyes narrowed and his tongue slid over his lower lip. "Hope you don't have any plans tonight," he cautioned, adjusting himself in the tight jeans.

Whatever response Lisa might've made was interrupted by the deep resonance of Declan's now-familiar voice.

"Sorry to keep you both waiting. Braden," he smiled, shaking Braden's hand. Then he turned sexy brown eyes on Lisa and her mouth went dry. "And Lisa, I presume," he took her hand in his big, warm one. "Declan Reece. Great to finally meet you both," he said, releasing Lisa's hand a second later than custom would dictate.

Declan was a bit taller than Braden, with dark, wavy hair that brushed his collar, and sprinkles of silver in the day-old scruff on his strong jaw. He smiled frequently and with his whole face, carving deep creases in his cheeks and crinkling his eyes. It undoubtedly contributed to his success. Charming and casual in dark jeans and a blazer, he reminded Lisa of the prototypical college professor every coed has a crush on.

He laid drawings on a long table. "Lisa, I know Ivy sent you the storyboards, but I want to look at them with you to make sure we're on the same page."

"Sounds good," she said, mentally giving the finger to office supplies everywhere.

"Initially, we were going for something a lot more straightforward. More like what the client has done previously, but using fresh faces." He looked from Braden to Lisa and smiled. "After speaking with Braden last week, I looked more closely at his pictures and all your other work, Lisa, and pitched this variation of the concept."

She nodded. As expected, the storyboard sketches of a shirtless male body were more than a little similar to many of Lisa's shots of Braden. When Natalie reviewed their contracts prior to signing she had insisted Lisa be paid an additional bonus for concept creation, and Declan readily agreed.

"I really respond to the whole 'what are you hiding, what am I not seeing' thing in your work... how it sucks you into the image, so let's teeter on that edge as much as possible. All right?" He studied her face with calm intensity, like he truly wanted to know that she was okay with his suggestions. It boosted her confidence. Not only was she about to do a photo shoot for a major brand and a huge agency, she'd gotten the job because her client actually recognized what set her work apart and saw value in that.

"It's more than okay. It's perfect." Lisa grinned so hard her face hurt. How ironic that after years of struggle, she was finally getting paid well for something she would happily do for free.

They discussed which poses to start with, then Braden stood on his mark and Lisa started setting up the lighting. Declan was chatting amiably with them both when Ivy arrived with a craft services cart. He snagged two bottles of water, handing one to Lisa then tossing the other to Braden, who snatched it out of the air.

"Thanks, man."

Declan opened a bottle for himself and settled into a folding chair. "Let me know if you need anything. Bathrooms are down the hall to the left, and feel free to plug into the speaker there if you want music."

When Lisa was satisfied with her light meter's findings, she sent Braden to the restroom. "You probably should go before we get started." He gave her an odd look as he walked out, and she cringed when she realized how much she had sounded like a mom.

"Known him a while, huh?" Declan chuckled.

"He used to babysit my son, and my ex left me for his mom." Then she laughed. "Wow, that sounded flippant, didn't it?"

"A little." His eyes crinkled as he considered her. "But healthy-flippant."

She uncapped her water. "I'm a few years past basket-case-flippant."

"Good to know," he murmured, sending a frisson of tingly awareness through her.

They heard laughter as Braden returned with Kimani. The stylist sent him back to his mark, then made minor adjustments to his hair and wardrobe. She moved the sides of his open shirt to fully expose one side of his chest while barely covering his other nipple.

"Now unbutton your jeans and tug 'em down a little bit, handsome," Kimani ordered.

"I thought you'd never ask," he teased and complied.

"A little lower... all the ladies wanna see those V-cuts you work so hard for."

He looked past Kimani to Lisa as he worked the jeans further down his narrow hips.

Emotions in turmoil, Lisa took a deep drink of water and almost did a spit-take when Kimani squeaked, "Whoa, baby -- that's enough. We only want the rainbow, not the pot of gold."

The atmosphere was light as they shot over the next couple hours. Declan occasionally gave input or direction, but was always considerate. He had Lisa recreate many of the shots from her first session with Braden, but better, since his beautiful face wasn't cropped out of these. She and Braden were confident they could defend their working relationship if Vance and Elena ever found out Lisa was the photographer on this job.

When they broke for lunch, Lisa took her sandwich to an empty table and popped the memory card into her laptop. The thumbnails had just come up when Declan slid onto the seat beside her. Her breath caught as his hard thigh brushed against hers.

"Mind if I look, too?"

"Oh. Well, um..." Glancing at his face, she saw respect and what appeared to be warm interest. She would think about the why of it later, but kept her thigh where it would continue to feel the heat of his. "I was gonna pull the weeds before showing you, but I don't mind if you don't." The first few shots were good, although Braden started out a little stiff. As soon as he relaxed, though, every one was excellent. Declan smirked and called over to Braden, "You are one ugly son-of-a-bitch, my friend."

Braden shot back, "You're pretty ugly yourself, boss. Maybe you should be the one dropping trou for the camera."

Lisa decided she would be totally fine with that.

As she scrolled to the next shot Declan shoved a hand through his hair, messing the dark waves and grumbled, "Shit. It's gonna suck trying to narrow these down."

Lisa beamed. "I've never been so happy to hear a client complain."

His lip quirked in a little smile as his eyes flicked over her face. "I'm not complaining."

After lunch, Kimani had Braden change into a faded indigo T-shirt. The soft cotton clung in all the right places, and the color she chose did sinful things for his eyes.

Ivy's phone buzzed with a text. "Hey Dec, I've gotta run upstairs for a minute. Andie's here to drop off some wardrobe."

"Tell her to come down and say hi." Declan turned to Lisa, "Andie's the other new model. We shot her stuff last week..." His voice trailed off as he apparently got caught up in a train of thought.

Braden got on his mark so Lisa could adjust the lighting. They hadn't had time alone all day and though they tried to communicate with their eyes, it did nothing but make them laugh.

Lisa checked the light meter and snapped a few test shots, leaning to the side when Declan looked at the viewfinder over her shoulder.

Braden drawled, "Yo, Declan, you want me to drop my drawers again?"

"With all my heart," Declan deadpanned.

Lisa's laugh got a little stuck in her throat as she watched Braden work the jeans down.

"Look what I found..." Ivy came in singing, tugging a young brunette by the hand. In track pants and a tank top, with no makeup and her hair in a messy bun, Andie was naturally gorgeous. She hugged Kimani and Declan, who both seemed genuinely happy to see her.

Declan introduced her to Lisa first, then Braden. When Braden shook the girl's hand, Lisa tamped down a misguided pang of jealousy. They looked beautiful together.

Ivy appeared beside Lisa and chuckled. "Could those two be any better looking?"

Lisa shook her head and smiled, thankful for the camaraderie. "Andie seems sweet. Guess I expected a girl who looks like that to be more of a diva."

"No, not at all. She played volleyball in the last Summer Olympics; that's where she got the ridiculous body. I think she's in grad school, now."

When Ivy left to take a call, Declan joined Lisa in watching Braden chat amiably with Andie. He indicated her camera and asked, "May I?"

"Be my guest." She stepped aside as he looked through the viewfinder.

When he straightened, he leaned close and quietly asked, "Do you see what I see?"

She took a deep breath and schooled her face and voice not to reveal any emotion as she murmured back, "What? That they look like they were made for each other?"

"Yeah, that." He gave her a crinkly-eyed smile. Then, watching her closely he asked in a low voice, "While she's here, would you mind taking some test shots of the two of them together?"

"Of course not. I'd be happy to." She hoped she sounded sincere.

Lisa pretended to check settings on her camera while Declan discussed the idea with Andie and Braden. She tried unsuccessfully to tune them out after she heard him ask whether they would be comfortable mimicking foreplay. Since nobody left the studio after that, she assumed their answers were affirmative.

When Kimani took Andie for a quick wardrobe change and hair styling, and Declan conferred with Ivy about updating contracts, Braden stole a private moment with Lisa.

"You sure you're okay with this?" He looked worried.

"I'm sure," she said, trying to convince them both. "It's not porn for Chrissake."

He chuckled. "No, but it's not the JC Penney catalogue, either."

They were both right, although the brief photo session certainly skewed more toward the porn side of the spectrum.

Andie had changed into a pair of ass-hugging jeans and a fitted t-shirt. Her breasts were of average size, proportionate to the rest of her athlete's body. If she wore a bra, it wasn't evident. Her dark brown hair hung in shiny waves almost to her waist.

Since Lisa was new to photographing couples, Declan gave most of the direction. First, he had Braden and Andie stand close, laughing together without touching. Then he had Braden pick Andie up in a bear hug and spin her around, both laughing. Lisa knew the pictures would be cute and sexy, and was proud of herself for not feeling jealous.

That pride was short-lived.

"Braden, don't put her down, yet," Declan said. "Hold her tight against you and I want you to look in each other's eyes... good... and now let her slide down your body-- slower, so Lisa can get the shots... nice. Lisa, how's it look to you?"

It looks like Andie's perky tits with their tight little nipples are brushing the part of Braden's chest I most enjoy licking, thanks for asking.

She ignored the twist in her gut. "It looks great. Really great."

Declan continued, "Andie, hold his face in both hands and lean in like you're about to kiss him... Perfect. Now Braden, hook your thumbs under the hem of her shirt, so it lifts and we see your hands on her bare ribcage as she slides the rest of the way down... Not too fast. Yeah, just like that..."

Lisa's hand was unsteady on the camera, and she gave thanks for the stability of tripods.

Chapter Seventeen

LISA'S PHONE RANG and she glanced at Braden's truck in her rearview before answering.

"You did great today," she said. "Declan seemed really happy."

He grunted. "Yeah. Hard to ignore the irony that once again, my success has nothing to do with my mind."

"It's a means to an end." She couldn't help teasing him a little, "I know it must've been torture, but it'll go a long way toward paying for med school."

"Was it torture for you, too?"

"Nah, just another day at the office." She was still reeling from the infusion of jealousy and lust with a shot of potent chemistry on the side. And she sounded it.

"You going straight home?" His voice was rough.

"Yes."

"Good," he said darkly before disconnecting.

Lisa pulled into the garage as Braden parked at the curb. She was barely out of the car when he grabbed her and shoved the door shut. He pressed her back, trapping her there with his big body as he took her mouth in a bruising kiss. Lisa's phone began ringing in her handbag, the muted tone easily ignored. She dropped the bag and ran both hands up his shirt, desperate to touch the warm, smooth skin of his chest and to erase the mental image of Andie's pert nipples pressed against him.

Lisa didn't realize her hips had been moving until he lifted her and wrapped her legs around his ass so she could hump him properly. Somewhere in the back of her mind, she was aware that she was grinding on him in her open garage, but her pussy was so wet and needy, she just didn't fucking care.

One strong hand slid under her ass, supporting her, while the other shoved her shirt and bra up, exposing her swollen breasts to his hungry mouth. His wicked tongue flicked over her nipples until they were harder than Lisa had ever felt them. Then he gently bit down on one tight peak then the other, tugging and elongating until she felt every pull on her clit.

The muffled sound of her ringing phone registered and she remembered where they were. "Inside."

"Yeah..." He held her up with one hand and started to work his jeans open with the other.

"In the *house*," she panted.

He grunted agreement and carried her inside, punching the button to close the garage before kicking the door shut.

"Bedroom's too far." He tumbled them to the floor in the hallway and shoved his jeans past his hips. "I can't wait."

"Me neither." She shucked her jeans and straddled him. Her shirt and bra were still up near her neck, and even as she ground herself against him she felt the urge to cover herself. He stared at her with long-lidded eyes and filled his hands with her breasts. "Sorry they're not as perky as you're used to now," she goaded.

Lifting his hips so Lisa's knees were off the floor and there was no mistaking how hard he was, he scowled. "Do you hear me complaining?"

"Of course not," she smirked. "You're about to get laid."

He grabbed her arms hard enough to leave red marks. "Is that all you think this is?" In a flash, he slipped out from under her and pushed her belly-down on the rug, holding her in place with a tight fist in her hair. She tried to lift her ass and he pressed her back down until her mons hit the floor. The fat head of his cock nudged her wet entrance, and he easily sank balls-deep. At her moan, he growled, "You like that? I like it, but of course any hole will do for me."

"That's not what I meant," she panted, trying again to push up.

He rose up on his knees and squeezed her ass cheeks with punishing hands, still holding her flat on the floor as he plowed into her again and again. "Then what *did* you mean?"

"It was hard to see you with her. Touching her."

"You mean, it was hard to see me doing my job?" He pulled out until just the tip of his cock connected them. Flexing his hips, he teased them both with slow, shallow thrusts. "The job I'll be doing again soon, only with less clothing?"

"Yes," she gasped, so wet, she could hear it each time he moved in her.

He grabbed her hands and held them tight against the floor over her head. "Since we're being honest, I don't like the way Declan looks at you." He reared back and drove his cock in to the hilt. "And I don't like the way he talks to you." He pulled out and slammed back in. "And I don't like the way you look at him and talk to him, either."

Lisa couldn't think straight to respond, as he'd started fucking her fast and deep, hitting her sweet spot with each stroke as he drilled her into the floor. He corkscrewed his hips and his thick base brushed her distended clit. The orgasm hit her long and hard. Wave after wave rolled through her, milking his iron-hard cock and dragging him over the edge with her.

For long minutes, they lay sweaty and panting on the hallway rug. When Braden roused himself enough to refasten his jeans, Lisa went to the bathroom to clean up.

She'd never had angry, jealous sex before. It was wild and almost primitive. But although she'd had one of the most intense orgasms of her life, she didn't like the way she felt now. Unsettled. She had no claim to jealousy, because she had no future with Braden. And he was right; much as she tried to hide it, she was attracted to Declan. She dreaded the conversation she and Braden clearly needed to have. After straightening her clothes and giving up on her just-got-fucked hair, Lisa knew she couldn't hide in the bathroom any longer.

She found him in the hall where she'd left him; a haunted look on his face. As soon as he saw her, he grabbed her in a fierce hug. "I'm sorry. I'm so sorry," he whispered into her hair.

And then a familiar voice said, "Not really what I had in mind when I asked you to help out around the house, *bro*."

"Jake!" she gasped, pushing Braden away. "You're home early. What happened?" He looked to have grown an inch in the month and a half since she had seen him, but his face was boyish as ever. He held his big duffel bag between them, blocking her attempt at a hug.

"Dad got in an argument with the camp." He glared at Braden. "He was surprised to see *your* truck out front."

"He was about to leave," Lisa said, begging him with her eyes to do just that.

Braden started to speak, but Jake cut him off with a harsh laugh. "Guess I should've expected this would happen, knowing you."

"Honey, go put your bag down and I'll make you something to eat."

Jake ignored her and sneered at Braden. "Right, Player?"

"Enough!" Lisa got between them, but the taller young men simply continued to face off over her head.

Braden's face tightened with anger. "You don't know what you're talking about, Jake."

"Fuck you, Brady. Well, never mind. Looks like my mom already did."

Lisa jumped out of the way as Braden slammed Jake against the wall. "Don't talk about her like that," he snarled. "Have some respect."

Face pressed next to the thermostat, Jake laughed mirthlessly, "Now that's funny."

No, she thought. *None of this was funny.*

Jake had to feel horribly betrayed to discover that two people he loved and respected had been carrying on an illicit relationship. She knew all too well how he felt, and it killed her to know she was the cause.

She felt even worse when she realized Vance and Elena could find out. Vance would give her a ration of shit about it despite not having a leg to stand on, and Elena would make Braden's life a living hell as long as he lived with them. What did Vance think was the reason

Braden's truck was out front? Had Jake explained that he'd asked Braden to help around the house? She itched to ask, but this wasn't the time.

Jake struggled to push Braden off him, and Lisa realized she had been standing there like an idiot hugging herself. She needed to take control before one of them got hurt. With a light touch on Braden's shoulder, she murmured, "You should go."

"You heard her, Player, get out of here," Jake spat.

"I'm sorry you found out like this, Jake, but it's not what you think." Braden released him and backed away, out of punching range. "I love her."

Lisa's hand fell over her mouth. *No, he can't mean that. He only said it for Jake's benefit, right?*

Then Braden flicked those stormy eyes to hers and broke her heart.

That long-overdue conversation was going to be harder than she thought.

Chapter Eighteen

HE LOVED HER.

Shit.

When this whole thing began, Lisa expected they'd have some fun then Braden would leave her devastated. It never crossed her mind that she'd be the one to end it.

And she *would* end it. Today.

However, that difficult conversation couldn't happen until Braden came out of Jake's room. She was trying not to pace a threadbare path in the hallway rug, but they had been in there a while.

After Braden struck her mute with his misguided declaration, Jake had said some more unflattering things about them both and shut himself in his bedroom. Braden followed him in and for the last fifteen minutes all she had heard were muffled, occasionally-raised voices.

As Jake's mom, she should have been the one in there talking to him. On the other hand, Jake felt most betrayed by Braden, so maybe Braden had a better chance at getting through to him.

To say she felt helpless was an understatement.

From inside Jake's room, she heard the murmur of Braden's calm voice and a yelled response from Jake. Suddenly, the door flung open and Jake stormed out with Braden right behind him.

The next minute was a blur, it all happened so fast.

Before Lisa could utter a word, Braden stopped Jake with a hand on his shoulder and Jake spun around to punch him. He had been aiming for Braden's jaw, but Braden ducked and Jake's fist made loud, cracking contact with the wooden door jamb.

At her son's howl of pain and anger, Lisa shoved her way between them. "Cut it out!"

Jake's arm shot past her and he punched Braden's bad shoulder. Both young men grunted in pain.

She put her hands on their chests to keep them apart. "Enough!" Not that they were going anywhere.

"God dammit," Braden spat.

Jake shook out his hand, then cradled it against his belly. "Serves you right, you dick."

Braden rubbed his shoulder. "Nice shot, though."

"Shut up, asshole."

Lisa let her hand drop from Braden's chest. "You should go," she said quietly.

His look told her he disagreed, but he nodded and headed toward the door.

She touched Jake's hand and he winced. "It still hurts?"

"What'd you expect?" He snapped. "I just punched a wall."

"Guess I expected you to be smart enough not to punch a wall." She gently prodded until he let her look at his hand. It was already turning purple and swelling.

Braden reappeared. "Sorry. Think I left my keys in Jake's room."

Lisa hardly noticed him passing by, as Jake was beginning to freak out, staring at his hand with alarm. "What if I broke it?" He panicked. "I won't be able to pitch when the season starts."

"We'd better go have it x-rayed," Lisa sighed.

Braden came out, shoving his keys in his pocket. He approached Jake cautiously, like one would an injured animal. "Mind if I take a look?"

Jake gave him a venomous glare, but Lisa interrupted whatever insult he had planned. "Thank you, Braden."

They moved into the kitchen where the lighting was better. Jake and Braden sat at the table, while Lisa made iced tea as an alternative to hovering.

Jake allowed Braden to examine his hand, but he kept his eyes averted, scowling out the window. He winced once or twice, but Braden had a gentle touch.

"Make a loose fist for me... Good. That's good. You've got all your knuckles, see? Sometimes, this one kind of disappears after a punch. Then you can be pretty sure you've got a break. Do you have any numbness or tingling?"

"No, but my wrist hurts like hell." He glared at Braden. "You don't have to look so happy about it."

Lisa was relieved when Braden chuckled, "Sorry, but pain is better than numbness with this kind of injury."

"So you think I'll be able to pitch?" Jake asked hopefully.

"Yeah. You jacked up the joints, but I doubt you've done any permanent damage." He carefully turned Jake's hand over. "There's swelling here around the joint and it's already starting to bruise... I'd say you've sprained your wrist, young man," he concluded in a cartoonishly-serious voice.

To Lisa's amazement, Jake grinned. It was as if the fight had never happened.

"Keep it elevated." Braden rested the injured hand against Jake's opposite shoulder. "I'm gonna make you an ice dip, then I'll show you how to wrap it up." His manner was calm and confident. He was so clearly meant to be a doctor.

While Lisa dug through drawers to find an elastic bandage, Braden filled the sink with ice water. "Okay, now you're gonna dunk your whole arm in up to the elbow..." He helped Jake lower his arm into the icy water. "Hold it there for five or ten seconds at a time."

Jake winced. "That's unpleasant."

"In and out for two hours," Braden continued. "You'll want to do it for the next few days." He took the bandage from Lisa and showed her how to wrap Jake's injured hand by having her practice on his good one.

"So we don't need to have it x-rayed?" she confirmed.

"Not unless there's a sharp pain or new swelling or bruising," he said, addressing Jake. "Rest it for at least two days. Keep it wrapped when you're not ice-dipping. And you wanna hold it above your heart to keep the swelling down. I've got a couple slings at home. I'll bring one by later."

"Thank you, Braden," Lisa said, relieved. His bedside manner worked wonders for worried moms, too.

He gave her a rueful smile, then watched as Jake continued to dip his arm in the frigid water. "Just like that, keep it up. You've only got another hour and fifty-five minutes to go," he grinned.

Lisa laughed when Jake scowled at him.

Braden palmed his keys and Lisa opened the kitchen door. As he walked out, his eyes were full of things he couldn't say.

"Hey Brady," Jake called, stopping him. "Thanks, bro."

"Anytime, bro," Braden smiled and left, closing the door behind him.

Lisa straightened her spine and reminded herself that she was the adult in the house before turning back to her son. She leaned on the counter beside the sink and watched him dip his arm in the icy water. After long minutes of silence, she had to say something.

"So."

"So," he repeated without looking at her.

"I'm sorry you had to leave camp early."

He snorted. "I'm sure you are."

"We're just good friends," she sighed.

He squinted at her, disbelieving. "Is that why he said he loves you?"

She shook her head. "I don't know why he said that."

"So you don't love him?"

"Not the way you're thinking, no." She was relieved to know it was the truth.

He went quiet, studying his swollen wrist as it went in and out of the water. Eventually, he asked, "Was he nice to you?"

Sweet boy. "Yes. He took care of the yard and tried to help me get in touch with your dad about the camp payment. He was very nice to me."

"That's good." He looked pensive again.

"Jake, I don't want you to be uncomfortable, so let's talk it all out. Is there anything else you want to--"

"Nope," he cut her off with almost-comical finality, and they both laughed.

Despite their horribly-awkward and unexpected reunion, Lisa and Jake ended up having a nice evening. He told her about camp and complained about coming home early, but ultimately he seemed happy to sleep in his own room.

Lisa was happy to close herself in *her* own room, too. Although, when she was finally alone with her thoughts they were a jumbled mess.

Jake's home... god that could've been a much bigger disaster.

Braden can't love me.

Fuck. Hate that I'm going to hurt him.

Hated seeing him with Andie...

He did a great job, though.

She smiled to herself, looking back on the exciting day. The pictures would be fantastic, she knew.

So proud and happy... and Declan.

Holy lord. Declan.

He wasn't beautiful like Braden, although he was definitely a very attractive man.

Magnetic. That's what he is.

As she sifted through mental snapshots of his sexy smile, her skin came alive again as she remembered how it felt to be near him. An insistent throb started between her legs.

Absolutely not.

What's on T.V.?

Maybe it was out of respect for Braden or maybe she worried it would make her a horrible person, but she felt guilty enough about her attraction to Declan; she refused to think about him while getting herself off.

So it was good timing -- or bad, or just fortuitous -- when Braden pinged.

Hey.

Hey, she tapped back. She was still resolved to end things with him. Unfortunately, having Jake home early pretty much put the kibosh on private conversation. Breaking it off via text wasn't her first choice, but she might not have another. She typed and erased a few attempts before he buzzed again.

Jake ok?

That was a broad question. She opted to address the easy part. *Yup. He did the ice-dip for two hours. Stopped complaining halfway thru when he went numb. :)*

LOL. He's got it in the sling now?

Yes and thanks again for dropping it off.

Her phone indicated he was typing... then not... then typing again... eventually buzzing in with, *Any excuse to see you.*

Lisa winced. The bastard didn't even use a smiley. He wasn't gonna make this easy. She typed out a response -- slowly, so she wouldn't have to backspace over most of it.

Can you come by tomorrow? Jake will be at a friend's house and we need to talk.

Her phone indicated he read her text immediately. She watched the screen until it went dark two minutes later. Braden was smart. He'd know why she wanted to talk. Fuck, she really didn't want to see those eyes filled with hurt. She was a goddamned idiot to have gotten involved with him.

Finally, her phone buzzed again. *This about what I said earlier?*

In part, yes.

OK, but just so you know... I meant it and I'm not taking it back.

Chapter Nineteen

BRADEN SHOWED UP after she had spent hours looking at him. Sorting through hundreds of gorgeous photos from the Allister & Hitch session, Lisa knew she was right to break things off. The shots of him with Andie settled it. Thanks to Braden, she now felt beautiful and comfortable in her own skin, but that skin would never look like a college girl's again.

It was a surprise to realize she was okay with that.

She was excited to test her new wings as a confident forty-one year-old woman. But first...

"You wanted to see me, Ms. Taylor?" His half-grin was sexy as always, but the vulnerable look in his eye made him seem more boy than man.

"Thanks for coming." She stepped aside to let him in, knowing even a small hug would send the wrong message. "Want a beer?"

"I'd take some iced tea if you've got it." He sat at the kitchen table and nervously bounced his knee, watching as she poured two glasses.

Avoiding any chance that their hands might touch, she set his on the table in front of him. He thanked her and sipped as she struggled to find the right words.

"So um, yesterday was a nightmare. I still can't believe Jake tried to punch you. Thanks again for taking care of him."

"Least I could do since he was nice enough to miss," he grinned. "How did the wrist look today?"

"Better. The color is hideous, but it's much less swollen." With a chuckle she added, "I made him do the ice dip again before he went to his friend's house." Her eye-roll indicated how much Jake complained about the treatment.

He shook his head. "Not the best patient, that kid."

"Nope. He did have a great doctor, though," she said pointedly.

A dimple flashed briefly before he sobered. "And is that doctor by any chance still involved with his patient's mom?"

"Braden," she sighed and met his sad, gorgeous eyes. "Even if we somehow kept seeing each other now that everyone's home, you'll be leaving to start med school soon."

"About that..." His eyes darted away in a flash of guilt, then returned to hers full of resolve. "What's the point of spending all the time and money on med school? I've got a good career going, now."

Lisa didn't even have to ask what Elena's reaction was when she'd heard about his modeling gig. She had been friends with his mother long enough to know Elena would be ecstatic about her son's perceived fame and fortune.

As always, it seemed Lisa was alone in recognizing Braden's nonphysical attributes. And as always, it broke her heart.

"Yes," she finally responded. "You may be on your way to a successful career, but you won't find it fulfilling. You'll spend the rest of your life in that cage where no one looks beyond your face and body."

"I know," he nodded. "You're the only one who ever has. That's why I love you."

"Braden..." She had to hug him, then, but made it quick so as not to send mixed messages. When she pulled back, his eyes were wet and she was blinking back tears of her own. "We'll always be friends and I'll always love you." She felt a tear slip out and wiped it with the heel of her hand. "Go to med school. Be the smart guy who also happens to be attractive, instead of the hot guy who just happens to have a brain. Date women your own age who appreciate who you really are -- you'll find them, I promise," she added, smiling at his skeptical look. "Let me take what you've given me and taught me about myself and experience the world like that for a while."

A tear slid down his cheek and opened the floodgates on hers.

She forced herself to continue before her throat closed up. "Maybe we'll come back to each other one day. But I hope not. I hope you find someone who deserves you and loves *all* of you; someone you can build a long life with."

Without warning he pulled her into a tight bear hug, murmuring into her hair, "I know you're right. I hate it, but I know you're right." He held her a long moment and took a shaky breath. "I really do love you, though."

"I really do love you, too." She hugged him back just as tightly, drenching his shirt with her tears.

* * *

Getting on with her life was easier said than done. She spent a few mopey days in the same t-shirt and sweats, finally perking up when Braden texted that he had sent off his med school applications.

Happy that he was moving forward, she had kicked herself in the ass to do the same. The result of said ass-kicking subsequently led to her staring into her closet for the last half-hour. She had gone from early to late and was still wearing a towel.

Natalie answered on the first ring, thank god. "Hey, Lise. What's up?"

"You've been to Davio's. What should I wear?"

"Depends." Natalie's grin carried through the airwaves. "Business or pleasure?"

Lisa felt her face heat. "Just a planning meeting with the Creative Director." She tried to sound casual, having already gotten an earful after telling Nat about the sexy and age-appropriate Declan.

"Oh, I can imagine what he's planning," her friend chuckled. "Don't mind me. As usual, I'm overworked and undersexed."

With Natalie's help, she decided on a pair of fitted charcoal pants and a lightweight, powder blue sweater that skimmed her curves and had a keyhole neckline which revealed a shadowy hint of cleavage. She was going for professional-but-sexy, and she nailed it.

Declan was waiting at the table when she arrived. He stood to greet her, looking charmingly edible in a black blazer over a crisp, white shirt unbuttoned against the tanned skin of his neck.

"Am I late? Hope you haven't been waiting long," she said as his warm lips brushed her cheek. His dark, wavy hair smelled fresh and tickled her nose.

He held out her chair. "Nope. I was early," he grinned. "You're right on time."

They ordered a bottle of wine and discussed the previous photo session. Lisa had sent him her favorite shots with some rough editing, and he was enthusiastic about them.

After the waiter brought their dinners, Declan described the shots he loved best and why. He told her which ones he thought he would use in small print ads, and which he envisioned on billboards and city busses.

Lisa couldn't stifle her grin. "Wow... That's...wow. I've been so focused on the work, I hadn't thought that far ahead."

Declan chuckled, enjoying her excitement. "Well then, you can think about this: if the session with Braden and Andie goes as well as I expect, I'm planning a giant ad on the 9000 building on Sunset in LA, and we'll probably buy a screen in Times Square."

"Holy shit." She downed the rest of her wine. "That's no pressure," she laughed.

He refilled her glass. "It shouldn't be. You do great work."

"Thank you, but Stevie Wonder could take great pictures of those two."

Ignoring her brush-off of his compliment, he rubbed his jaw and studied her through narrowed eyes. "You sure do have a lot of interesting pictures of Braden in your portfolio."

She chuckled and glanced away. "Yeah, it took me a little while to get the hang of working with a human."

"Don't self-deprecate," he frowned. "You're a brilliant photographer. And Braden seemed surprisingly relaxed for a first-time model, especially since you shot him nude." One dark eyebrow lifted. "He must be very comfortable with you."

Lisa knew what he was asking without asking. She didn't want to lie, so she avoided the question. "We've known each other a long time."

His cheek scrunched in a lopsided smile that heated her. Or maybe it was the wine. "Would you be offended if I said you're cute when you blush?"

It was definitely not the wine. "Of course not. I'm not blushing." Her face felt hot. "It's just a little warm in here..." To her relief, he was kind enough not to mention the woman at the next table pulling on a sweater.

"My mistake," he conceded, though his eyes twinkled with humor as the wait staff cleared the table and refilled their glasses.

Lisa couldn't help thinking there was something impossibly sexy about a man who laughed a lot. Especially if that man happened to have gorgeous, long-lashed brown eyes that crinkled expressively, and a smile that carved deep grooves in the hollows of his cheeks.

When they were alone again, she pulled out her tablet and attempted to steer the subject to safer ground. "I've got the test shots here, if you'd like to go through them."

Declan ignored that and picked up the thread of the conversation she was trying not to have. "For the record, I've got no issue with it, professionally. He's a great looking kid; I don't blame you." His dark-coffee eyes touched her face like a caress. "And I definitely don't blame *him*."

The look he gave her caused delicious flutters low in her belly. She calmed them down with a swig of wine. "I'm a little confused... Was that a reprimand or the strangest compliment ever?"

His deep-voiced laugh made her skin tingle. "It was a fucked-up compliment." He ran a hand through his hair, further rumpling it in his embarrassment. "Sorry if I'm being nosy. Just determining whether I should express my interest or keep it to myself."

"Oh." She knew she was blushing again, so she covered with a brazen smirk. "Well, let me know what you decide."

"I'll do that," he grinned, eyes crinkling.

Tapping a finger on her tablet, Lisa asked, "Should I put this away, or do you want to look through the shots?"

He quirked his lip and gave a little shrug. "Might as well. Don't want you accusing me of having ulterior motives for taking you to dinner."

"So, you didn't?"

"I absolutely did. But nobody likes accusations." She laughed and he nodded toward the tablet. "Let's see what we've got."

She pulled up the test shots and they scrolled through, discussing her vision for each of them. When they were done she closed that app, revealing her background picture of Jake in his baseball uniform. Before she could turn off the tablet, he touched her hand.

"Hang on. Is that your son?" He studied the photo, genuinely interested.

"Yeah, that's Jake. I took that after the playoffs last year. He's fifteen now."

"Good-looking kid. He looks like you, especially around the eyes."

"I can't believe you noticed that. Nobody ever does." Jake got his blue eyes from Vance, so it was rare for anyone to recognize his resemblance to Lisa. She put the tablet away. "Do you have kids?"

"Unfortunately, no." He topped off their glasses. "I got married back in my twenties, but we weren't ready for parenthood; we weren't even ready for marriage. Haven't gotten that close to serious again. Not yet, anyway," he added.

Before she could read much into that, he asked to hear more about Jake. She shared some funny stories about Jake as a little boy, some including Braden, and mentioned Vance as briefly as possible. They talked until the wine was gone and the tables around them were empty.

She thanked him for dinner as he walked her to her car.

"It was my pleasure." He gave her a sexy smile and opened the door for her.

Instead of getting in, she took a deep breath and looked up at him. "I think it's only fair to let you know you were right about Braden and me, but that's over. We're just good friends, now."

Declan's lip curved in a half-smile and his lashes lowered as he brushed a wayward curl from her cheek. His deep voice was gravelly when he murmured, "In that case, I'm interested." He stepped closer and pressed a warm, firm kiss on her mouth. When she softened, he slid his big hands under her hair and nibbled her lips until they opened for him.

The excellent wine they'd had with dinner tasted better on his tongue. She skimmed her hands over his wide shoulders and he pressed her back on the car, deepening the kiss. His hands cradled her face, holding her still while he took his time with her mouth. A familiar clench between her legs made her squirm, and she felt him harden against her belly.

They reluctantly pulled apart, both a little breathless. "I should let you go before I ravish you in the parking lot." The sinful rasp in his voice belied his droll choice of words.

"If you're trying to convince me to leave, you're doing a crap job," she whispered. Her hands traveled over the front of his shirt, exploring, and she discovered he was all lean muscle under there.

"We have a shoot coming up," he said roughly.

"I remember."

"With the potential for some complicated emotions," he added with an arched eyebrow.

"Yeah," she sighed and reluctantly withdrew her hands.

He licked his lips and his cheeks creased in a slow, panty-drenching smile. "It's not that I'm not dying to ravish you in the parking lot; I am. That's why I have to back off until the shoot wraps." He stroked a thumb along her collarbone right above the neckline of her sweater, then traced the keyhole cut-out, teasing her cleavage and igniting every erogenous zone she had. She whimpered and the light in his eyes said he knew exactly what he was doing to her, before he nudged her to get in the car, adding, "I like you and I don't want to fuck this up."

Chapter Twenty

LISA WAS NAKED. Declan wasn't. Neither were Braden and Andie. They were all in the studio for the shoot, but she was naked and everyone else was dressed for the North Pole. She wasn't embarrassed until they began laughing at her. Their amusement at her expense was shrill. Endless.

"Oh, *come on!*" She shut off the alarm, though it felt as if she'd only just set it. She had wrestled the blankets for hours last night, chasing sleep. Today was the shoot with Braden and Andie, and her brain had been on overdrive for days. Professionally, she couldn't wait to get started; it was a thrilling opportunity to work for as visible a brand as Allister & Hitch. Personally, however she was a mess of conflicting emotions. She dreaded seeing Braden kissing Andie in various states of undress. It was going to hurt, despite the fact that ending it was the right thing for both of them.

On the flip side, she couldn't get Declan's sexy voice out of her head. They had spoken a few times since their dinner; mostly work-related with a little flirting. Much as she itched to have her hands and mouth on him again, she was glad he'd insisted they wait until the shoot was behind them.

When Lisa got to the studio, Andie was in wardrobe and Braden was in Kimani's chair having his hair professionally mussed. He looked a little somber, but gave Lisa a wink in the mirror to let her know he was okay.

After chatting with Ivy over a few gulps of coffee, Lisa set up the lights and was tightening the foot of her tripod when Declan arrived.

She was getting used to the way his crooked smile made her feel like a girl with her first crush. Conversely, his low-murmured "good morning" was as intimate as if he had just awakened beside her. Her pussy responded with a clench and a damp "yes please."

"Good morning, yourself," she managed.

From then on, it was strictly business as they reviewed the shot list and gave last looks and wardrobe approval. Then Braden and Andie took their marks, Lisa tweaked the lighting, and it was time to work.

Allister & Hitch was known for its risqué advertising. To Lisa's relief they started the day with both models fully-dressed, albeit Andie was clearly braless under the thin white button-down. Declan directed Braden to hug Andie from behind and nuzzle her neck. Lisa kept the shutter going and let Declan call the shots.

She caught him watching her speculatively -- mindful of her past with Braden, she assumed, and checking that she was comfortable with where the shoot was going. It was crucial to her both personally and professionally that he never feel the need to do that again.

Time to rip off the Band-Aid.

Stepping out from behind the camera, she teased, "Jesus, Braden, she's not your grandmother. Look at her; she's gorgeous. Hold her like she's your girlfriend... someone you're intimate with."

Braden gave Lisa an inquisitive look and she nodded. After a moment, he flashed her that dimpled smile and she knew they had cleared the hurdle. Still pressed to Andie's back, his arms had been wrapped around her waist; now he moved one arm across her chest with his hand on her shoulder. His other hand splayed on her flat stomach.

"Better," Lisa said, feeling Declan's approval without having to look at him.

Andie rolled her eyes and snorted, "Not by much." She plucked Braden's hand off her shoulder and put it on her breast. "Hold that. It's a boob. I assume you've handled one before?" It jarred Lisa for a second, seeing his familiar hand on another woman's body, but Braden's laugh was contagious and instantly lightened her mood.

After that, Lisa took over most of the direction with only minimal input from Declan. She had Braden reach around and unbutton Andie's shirt from behind, resulting in some very hot images. Then Andie shrugged the shirt off a shoulder, and Braden slid one hand over her bared breast; the other dipped into the front of her jeans. Lisa smiled to herself. *He's a quick study, that kid.* They finished that set-up with the requisite "Topless Hugs Sell Jeans" shots in various standing and prone positions.

The models left to change and Lisa popped a fresh battery in her camera. She glanced at Declan when they had a minute of privacy. "Happy so far?"

"Very." His thick-lashed eyes narrowed at her. "Are *you* happy?"

She grinned up at him with bright eyes. "Yeah," she nodded. "I really am."

"Good." Brushing his knuckles down her cheek he added, "You should be." He put professional distance between them again, but they stood like that a long moment; saying a lot without speaking a word. When his buzzing phone popped their bubble, he gave her a hot-promising look, and went to coordinate placement of a bed for the next set-up.

Andie was the first to return from wardrobe. They had put her in A&H's "Cheeky" boyshort underwear, which hugged the top half of her firm round ass. Her pink t-shirt contrasted nicely with the sweet floral print of the panties.

Lisa waved her over. "Thanks for helping out before, getting Braden to loosen up."

"It's a tough job, but someone's gotta do it," Andie joked with a shrug. Then she glanced over her shoulder and asked, "Um, you're good friends with him, right? Do you know if he has a girlfriend?"

Lisa had kind of expected this. "He was seeing someone for a little while, but that's over now." She raised her eyebrows. "I assume this isn't just idle curiosity..."

"Not if he's single," Andie confided with a laugh. "He's freaking gorgeous."

"Yeah, he is." Feeling the need to protect him, she added, "He's smart, too."

The girl's face lit up. "I know!"

"You do?" Lisa hadn't expected *that*.

"When he heard I played in the Olympics he started talking about football, and I was like, 'Next!'" She pointed a thumb at the door. "But then he told me he's gonna go to med school, and, um... he, uh..."

Lisa looked up and saw Braden walking in wearing nothing but soft blue pajama pants that hung low on his hips. She gave Andie a little push, whispering, "Go on; ask him to grab a beer with you later." She was surprised when the girl hugged her before making a beeline for Braden.

Over the next couple hours, Lisa and Declan watched from behind her camera as the beautiful young couple rolled around on the bed and discovered each other. Their first kisses were tentative, but as they grew more comfortable those kisses flashed glimpses of tongue and wandering hands explored freely. They were beautiful together; sexy and playful. At one point, Braden tugged Andie's panties halfway down her butt and she screamed with laughter. When he sank his teeth into her plump, round ass, Kimani praised Jesus and Ivy fanned herself with an issue of *Cosmo*.

It all would have been bittersweet if Lisa hadn't felt Declan's heat at her back; his voice a low rumble in her ear. "Let me take you out tonight."

As it was, they never made it out of the studio.

By the time they wrapped, the rest of the building had emptied. Kimani and Ivy packed up and said their goodbyes. Braden and Andie left together, after they each hugged Lisa and whispered a private "thank you" in her ear. It was kind of adorable.

As Declan helped Lisa put away her equipment he said, "You were fantastic today."

"Thanks," she glowed. "I think we got some really good shots."

"I know we did. And I know they'll be amazing after you do your thing."

She chuckled as they sat to watch the thumbnails load on her laptop. "'My thing?'"

"Yeah. When you crop them and wave your magic wand so I only see what you want me to see." He stared at her with stark admiration. "It's like I'm looking through those gorgeous eyes of yours."

Lisa sucked in a breath at the answering response in her core. Declan understood and appreciated her work, and that thrilled her in every possible way. She was lost for words, so she kissed him.

It was meant to be a soft, sweet kiss. A closed-mouthed thank-you kiss. But after long days spent fantasizing about him, she couldn't keep her tongue from stealing a taste. He sat still as stone as she took his face in her hands and traced his smile lines with her thumbs. His eyes bored into hers with open wonder and restrained lust.

His jaw flexed under her fingers. "Are you sure?"

She swung one leg over both of his and sat on his lap, facing him. "I've never been more sure of anything in my life." And she had Braden to thank for it.

"I can wait," he rasped.

"I can't." She ground herself against his prominent erection, dug her fingers into his silky hair and pulled his hot mouth to hers.

He kissed her back ravenously, taking her mouth from every possible angle. His large hands spanned her waist, then skimmed their way up to cover her breasts. She sucked in a breath when her tight nipples scraped his palms.

With blooming confidence, Lisa pulled her shirt over her head and tossed it. Declan stared at her lush breasts swelling over the shelf bra she wore for him. He teased the top edge with a fingertip, brushing an areola where it peeked above the lace.

"Christ, you're gorgeous," he murmured, kissing a lazy, wet path between her breasts. His bristly jaw felt delicious against her tender skin.

She reached between them and tugged at his belt.

"Wait a second." He dropped a hand to hers, halting her progress but effectively pressing her palm against his hard length. "Let's get out of here."

"I'm happy here." She nipped his neck and squeezed his cock through his pants.

"We're on a folding chair."

"I don't mind." The part of him in her hand twitched in agreement. She slid her other hand into the hair at his nape and kissed him.

"I do." With an eye-crinkling smile, he stood and Lisa's feet hit the floor. "I'd feel cheap, later," he quipped and she gave a growly whine in response.

They both glanced over at the bed at the same time.

"Would that be weird?" she asked.

"Think that's up to you."

"Nothing really happened on it."

"It's set decoration," he reasoned.

"And next time can be in an actual bedroom."

"I'd hope so."

"So it's not weird," she concluded.

"Excellent." He scooped her up and she squealed when he dropped her on the bed. He leaned over her, thick lashes heavy as he gripped her chin in a strong hand and kissed her hard.

She reached for his belt again and he pulled her hands away, forcing them to the mattress over her head when she fought him. The position arched her back, pushing her breasts up to expose her nipples over the low-cut bra. His dark eyes raked over her and her pussy responded with a wet rush. She lifted her hips, mound grazing his hard length before he smirked and moved his crotch out of range.

"Let me, Declan," she groaned in frustration. "I want you."

His cheek creased in the sexy smile that fired up every nerve ending in her body. "I want you, too, gorgeous." He caught a nipple between his teeth and tugged, dragging the flat of his tongue across the sensitive tip. "But I won't let you rush this." He sucked her other nipple hard and released it, then teased the wet peak with thumb. "I was serious when I said I like you." With a look of carnal intent, he pressed moist lips to the soft sensitive skin above her navel. "And I'm not going to fuck this up."

If you enjoyed **Extreme Close-Up**,

look for Natalie's story
Over-Exposed

Book Two of the *PERSPECTIVES* Series

Coming Fall 2014

<u>About the Author</u>

JULIE JARET IS an American screenwriter with one feature film produced and some others on deck. Her alter-ego needed an outlet, so here we are.

Julie lives in the southeast U.S. with her sexy and supportive husband, two funny and beautiful kids, and one big doofus of a dog. She enjoys living vicariously through her fictional characters, often to the point of distraction... (Luckily, her hubby and kids know not to expect dinner at a certain time. Or at all.)

If reading *Extreme Close-Up* put you in a good mood, helped you plan your weekend, and/or caused mild to moderate swelling in your nether regions, please take a minute to leave an Amazon review. She'd truly appreciate it!

Connect with Julie Online

http://juliejaret.wordpress.com

https://twitter.com/JulieJaret

https://www.facebook.com/pages/Julie-Jaret-Author/
512928708815568

62928445R00075

Made in the USA
Middletown, DE
31 January 2018